Death By Stalking

A Josiah Reynolds Mystery

Abigail Keam

Worker Bee Press

ISBN 978 0 9979729 2 4
7 8 2019

Published in the USA

Worker Bee Press
P.O. Box 485
Nicholasville, KY 40340

Acknowledgments

Thanks to my editor, Heather McCurdy

Artwork by Cricket Press
www.cricket-press.com

Book jacket by Peter Keam
Author's photograph by Peter Keam

By Abigail Keam

Josiah Reynolds Mysteries
Death By A HoneyBee I
Death By Drowning II
Death By Bridle III
Death By Bourbon IV
Death By Lotto V
Death By Chocolate VI
Death By Haunting VII
Death By Derby VIII
Death by Design IX
Death By Malice X
Death By Drama XI
Death By Stalking XII

Mona Moon Mysteries
Murder Under A Blue Moon I
Murder Under A Blood Moon II
Murder Under A Bad Moon III

The Princess Maura Tales Fantasy Series
Wall Of Doom I
Wall Of Peril II
Wall Of Glory III
Wall Of Conquest IV
Wall Of Victory V

Last Chance For Love Series
Last Chance Motel I
Gasping For Air II
The Siren's Call III
Hard Landing IV
The Mermaid's Carol V

PROLOGUE

I can't get the sight out of my mind—that of her standing over his body holding a knife, which was dripping blood on the floor. When she turned, her dress was drenched in blood.

She looked at me and said, "I didn't do this. Josiah, you've got to believe me."

I rushed over, feeling for a pulse. "He's still alive. Call an ambulance!"

How could such a nice evening go so wrong?

It all began with those stupid chairs.

1

The squat, moustached man was perspiring heavily and mopped his neck with a crisp, monogrammed cotton handkerchief. He anxiously watched a dark-haired woman with patrician features turn over a Louis XV chair, which had been custom made for His Majesty's last mistress, Madame du Barry.

The chair had a sensuous medallion backrest and delicate fluted legs, sitting close to the ground and at an angle. The armless chair was designed with a voluptuous seat, short legs, and a sloped backrest. The sloped backrest accommodated mesdames and mademoiselles who fancied dresses with panniers, which allowed their dresses to expand three or even four feet in width at the hips, thus enabling court ladies to gracefully alight in their impossibly elaborate couture.

The young woman put on a jeweler's magnifying headlamp and meticulously scanned every square inch of the chair's bottom. "Uh-huh," she mumbled. "As I suspected."

The man grew increasingly nervous. "Qu'est-ce que c'est, Mademoiselle Asa?"

Asa threw off her headset and flipped the chair upright. "I'm very sorry, but I'm afraid this chair is a fake."

"That can't be!" exclaimed the curator of the museum. "Over a million US dollars was spent to purchase this chair. I had several experts authenticate it."

"You should get your fee back from them."

"Why should I believe you when other experts in eighteenth-century French furniture say this chair is one of the original twelve chairs made by Louis Delanois in 1769?"

"Because they are either lying or mistaken, but either way, the insurance company will not underwrite this chair after I submit my report."

"Mon Dieu! This you must not do."

"I am sorry, Monsieur Faucheux, but the proof is in the pudding."

Faucheux looked confused. "What does pudding have to do with this?"

Asa gave a ghost of a smile. "Let me explain. Do you agree that Louis Delanois was commissioned by King Louis XV to make twelve chairs for Madame du Barry?"

"Mais oui, Mademoiselle. Everyone knows that."

"We agree on this very important fact?"

"Certainement."

"Versailles is in possession of ten of the chairs, and a collector bought the other two chairs from the estate of André Meyer in 2001 so that accounts for all twelve." Asa shot a glance at the chair and looked up to meet the anxious stare of Monsieur Faucheux. "This is a fake. I can prove it. There are no tan lines for one thing. Wood from the eighteenth century would be more discolored. Also, its construction is too tight where two pieces of wood meet. The joints would be looser on a chair over two hundred years old."

"Simple conjecture on your part."

"Hmm," murmured Asa, not pleased at Monsieur Faucheux's stubbornness. She was not accustomed to having people, especially men, question her authority. "Sir, I recognize the handwriting on the label. It is the handwriting of a well-known forger. The label should be more distressed and faded. The forger has soaked it in tea to make the label look older. You can smell the lack of age on it. It doesn't smell musty."

Monsieur Faucheux wiped his forehead and patted his palms. His coloring was a bright cherry red.

"Would you please taste the medallion, Monsieur Faucheux?"

"You want me to eat the chair?"

"No, I want you to lick the wood. Please."

Looking dubiously at Asa, Monsieur Faucheux bent over and did as requested. "It tastes like, um, candy, perhaps licorice?"

"That is the final proof. Black licorice has been melted and rubbed into the wood to give it an aged and tarnished look. It's clever, but a dead giveaway. The chair is worth something as a fine reproduction, but far less than the money you paid for it. I'm very sorry."

Asa closed her briefcase and picked up her jacket. "The insurance company will bill you for my time. My final report will be mailed to you. Don't bother to see me out. I'll find my way. Again, I'm very sorry to be the bearer of such bad news."

She made her way out of the small inspection room, through the main gallery hall, and out onto the noisy street where she hailed a cab. Curators had been known to become violent, so she liked to make a quick exit when presenting bad news. After telling the cab driver to hurry to the airport, Asa called her employer and gave a report. She listened to new instructions that she was to fly to Lisbon and pick up a cache of diamonds.

"What is the origin of the diamonds?" Asa asked, listening intently to the answer. She didn't like what she heard. "Sorry, I don't move conflict diamonds. Get some other patsy." She hung up.

Before putting the phone in her pocket, she looked for any calls or texts from her mother, Josiah Reynolds. Nothing. She hadn't heard from her mother in two weeks. She had contacted Lady Elsmere, but neither she nor Charles had seen Josiah for several weeks either. When she finally got hold of Eunice Todd, her mother's business partner, Eunice reassured her that Josiah was fine, and she would tell her mother Asa had called, but Eunice sounded tentative. Asa wondered if her mother was in the hospital and had told everyone not to alert her.

There was only one way to find out.

No time for sightseeing in Paris, France.

Asa was going home.

2

I knew Asa was calling. I didn't want to talk to her. Asa was like a drill sergeant. Nag. Nag. Nag.

Oh, wait a minute. That's me. A little chuckle there, but it was true. I was avoiding her.

It wasn't just Asa. I didn't want to talk to anyone.

Here's another truth. I was depressed. Not the average middle-age "how did I get to be so old?" depression, but a ripe, bruised, fruity depression that sucked the life out of a person breath after breath. I was struggling—staggering like a sailor on an all-night drinking binge, in fact—not physically, but mentally. Let me tell you how it is.

I was, I mean, I am becoming unhinged.

My name is Josiah Louise Reynolds. I own a farm in the Bluegrass and live in an iconic mid-century house called the Butterfly. I make my living by selling honey, so you can say I'm a beekeeper. I would say I'm a bee guardian. I love my bees, and in this upside-down world of pesticides and backyard grass deserts, I do all I can to protect them. They need me.

I also board horses, and I am a partner with Eunice Todd in an event/catering business.

I was finally in the black each month. My animals were fat and happy. Clients gave rave reviews on the web. The farm was in good shape.

Things should be hunky dory, right? So why was I becoming unhinged?

Because my life sucked.

I guess I never fully recovered from my husband Brannon leaving me. Brannon lied to me. Cheated on me. Stole from me. Abandoned me. The man I loved bellowed that he hated me in the parking lot of Keeneland Race Course. What had I done to deserve such loathing from a man I had slept with for over twenty years? What was my big crime? What?

And then there was that nutcase of a cop stalking and pulling me off a cliff and leaving me with this busted-up body.

It's a wonder I still get out of bed in the morning.

But I do.

I dutifully wash my face, comb my hair, and put on clean clothes. I feed my animals, check the horses in the pastures, pay my bills, take my pills, and clean the Butterfly. I smile at appropriate pauses during conversations until I no longer listen and miss all the social cues, causing people to think I'm an odd duck.

Well, maybe I am an odd duck.

It was one thing for me to know I was sinking. I certainly didn't want the world to see me fumble the ball as well, so I retired from life.

I told Eunice I was not up to the event/catering business any longer and wanted out. I was grateful when she agreed to take over all the details and rent the Butterfly from me when she had a booking, refusing to dissolve our partnership.

"You'll snap out of this funk. Everything from the past few years is just catching up with you."

I didn't believe her words of cheer, but I knew she needed the money we made from renting out the Butterfly, so I was willing to do what Eunice wanted.

But what about what I wanted?

It seemed all the people who kept me on an even keel were gone. Meriah Caldwell won her custody battle for Emmeline, so Matt, my best friend, had packed up and moved to California to be near his child.

Asa closed her office in London but had come no nearer than New York. She might as well have stayed in London.

Now that Officer Kelly was a homicide detective, he never brought hot chocolate and donuts to my stand at the farmers' market.

My buddy Detective Goetz had moved to Florida. He had not called nor written once. I guess he's still mad that I turned him down. I agree with him that it's best we don't communicate.

I hadn't heard from my former boyfriend—young hot Choctaw Jake—in years, but I think of him from time to time. Fondly.

Franklin moved in with his brother Hunter, and they spend their time working on Wickliffe Manor.

Hunter had decided to sell the family estate and was heartbroken over the decision, but he was close to bankruptcy. Having no choice in the matter, he girded up his loins, so to speak, and was working at a frantic pace to make his ancestral home fit to sell.

Consequently, I saw neither Franklin nor Hunter unless I hopped in my car and drove to Wickliffe Manor, but I rarely went. It was hard to think that an estate with such an illustrious history, bad and good, was going to be sold and most likely carved into tiny one-acre lots with cheap housing.

Oh, don't get me wrong. Young couples have to buy starter homes somewhere. And don't forget my late husband Brannon and I made quite a bit of money on a housing development we did ourselves, but dismantling Wickliffe Manor and its land didn't feel right.

God wasn't making any more Bluegrass. Once the land was bulldozed, it was gone forever.

Enough of my preaching. You know how I feel about children, littering, and development of the land. I could go on ad nauseam, but there was a knock on the door.

Eunice had booked the Butterfly for the weekend, so Baby, my English Mastiff, and I had taken up residence in Matt's bungalow, which is located on my property.

Since Baby hadn't bothered to raise his head from his mammoth paws, I realized he knew the person at the door, so I opened it.

"Here you are!" There stood my favorite grande dame, Lady Elsmere, aka June Webster, wearing a vintage sixties blue and gray plaid dress suit with a strand of pearls. An old-fashioned plastic rain cap, fastened under her chin, covered her silver hair. I glanced up into the sky for pending rain. Not a cloud was to be seen.

Peering about the cottage's tidy yard, I asked, "What are you doing here?"

"Are you going to invite me in or keep me wobbling on my arthritic knees?"

I stepped out of the way as June shoved past me and promptly plopped down on Matt's couch.

"Where's Amelia?" I asked, referring to June's nurse and companion.

"I dispatched her on a little errand and scooted out the side door."

"Why? You could have called, and I would have come to see you."

"Would you have? I was under the impression you were absorbed in a little pity party."

"Why would you say that?"

June reached up and pinched my cheek as if I were a toddler. "Don't lie to me, Babycakes. I see all the telltale signs of a serious hissy fit. I've gone through several of them during my lifetime. I know what I see."

I started to tear up. "Oh, June. I don't know what's wrong. Everything upsets me. I'm confused and feel like bawling all the time."

"Every woman goes through this one time or another during her life."

"I just want to be left alone."

"Meaning you want me to go?"

"Well, actually, yes. I would like for you to leave, June."

She gave me a smile reserved for small children and dinner guests who didn't know which fork to use. "Not going to happen. You need to snap out of this funk."

"Oh, here it comes—the lecture. 'Just get on with it, Josiah. It's mind over matter. You can be happy if you put your mind to it.'" I spouted in a syrupy voice, making air quotes as I spoke. "What a load of crap! If I could click my heels together three times and *snap* out of the blue meanies, don't you think I would?"

"I agree."

"You do? Then why did you tell me to snap out of it?"

"To make you angry. Nothing motivates people like anger."

"It worked."

"Good. Now get some shoes on and bring this slimy monster with you," June said, nudging Baby with her Christian Louboutin shoe, which would have cost me a whole month's pay.

Baby made a puffing noise and rolled onto his other side, ignoring June and her pointed shoe.

"He doesn't like to be poked," I mentioned before slipping on some rubber flip-flops.

"What do you feed that thing?"

"That thing has a name," I said, huffing while trying to find a leash. I jerked my head up. "Oh, are you still trying to make me mad?"

June beamed a self-satisfied smile. "I'll wait outside. Don't forget to bring the dog." With that, she slammed the screen door behind her.

I put on a clean shirt and brushed my hair. Lately, I brush my teeth, but not my red hair. I could see the day coming when I wouldn't bother to brush my teeth either. Shaving my legs? Don't even go there. I looked in the mirror and saw a woman teetering on the brink of just not giving a damn anymore. How did June keep it together all the time?

Heading outside, I called to Baby. "Come on, big boy. We've been summoned."

Baby groaned, sleepily struggling to stand up on all fours. He glared at me as though saying, "I was having such a good dream. I had all the treats I desired, and

you weren't there telling me I couldn't eat them all."
He trotted outside, making complaining noises all the
way, with me following behind.

I searched for June and discovered her perched on
the passenger seat in my beat-up golf cart. I didn't see
the Bentley and wondered how she got here, but
pushed those thoughts aside, as I got in the driver's
seat while Baby jumped in the back, immediately sliding
his gigantic head over June's shoulder, wanting to be
petted.

She laughed and reached up to stroke Baby's nose.
"You're just a big baby, Baby."

I reached for a towel in the back of the cart to wipe
away the strands of drool hanging from Baby's mouth.
"Baby, sit down. You're getting June all grimy."

"Don't worry, Josiah. I don't care."

"For a woman who doesn't care about clothes, you
sure have a lot of threads in your closet."

Ignoring me, June suggested, "This cart is on its last
legs. You better get it replaced."

"Sandy Sloan shot it trying to kill me, and then Da-
rius shot it trying to save me. I'm lucky Matt got it to
run at all."

"How is our deliciously beautiful Matt?"

I sighed. "Settling in. Meriah is being difficult about
letting him see Emmeline."

"Doesn't he have a court order stating when he can
visit?"

"Yes, but Meriah keeps making excuses when Matt comes to pick Emmeline up."

"Like what?"

"She'll say Emmeline has a temperature—stuff like that." I fidgeted in my seat. "Can we talk about something else?"

"For instance?"

"How did you get over here? I don't see a car."

"I had Malcolm drop me off."

"For what purpose?"

"All of a sudden I need a reason to see one of my dearest friends?"

I gave June a "look."

June decided to fess up. "I got a telephone call less than an hour ago, so you and I are embarking on a mission of mercy."

"Who called?"

"Rosie."

"Oh, dear. What's happening now?"

"That Neanderthal has locked her in and won't let her out."

"No way!"

"We should be going. The police should be there by now." June gave me a hard look. "Doesn't it make you feel better knowing Rosie is having such a hard time with that monster?"

"I know this is terrible, but it does. However, I strongly sympathize."

"There is no better medicine for depression than helping someone else suffering from worse afflictions."

"I feel guilty."

"Don't. It's human nature."

"What's Baby for?"

"Baby is a deterrent. Gage is terrified of big dogs."

"Then let's go and save Rosie from the despicable troll at her gate."

June licked her lips and smiled. "Misery loves company."

"What was that?"

"Nothing. Just drive, mon amie. Just drive."

3

The golf cart rattled and lurched down my gravel driveway until we hit the smooth asphalt of Tates Creek Road. We drove a mile or two until we came to Wiley Road and made a left.

We were no longer in Fayette County, but in Jessamine County. We passed people mowing yards, weeding gardens, and tending to horses on their ten-acre mini-farms. They would look up and wave, recognizing Lady Elsmere, who waved back with little twists of her right hand like her friend, Queen Elizabeth II or "Lizzie" as June calls her. Personally, I think June has never met Queen Elizabeth, but the queen does board some of her horses in the Bluegrass, and they both run in the same circles since June had married an English lord.

Still, I rolled my eyes.

Finally, we reached the remotest part of the road where the real, working farms were. Scruffy farm dogs yapped at us as we skirted their territory, and I had to veer around an errant cow that had decided the middle of the blacktop road was as good a place to poop as any.

Welcome to the country.

I could feel Baby rise on all four paws in the back of the cart, snarling warnings to any dog venturing too close to our slow-moving vehicle. As soon as we reached the end of a farm's property line, its sentinel mutt would abruptly stop barking and give up the chase.

No longer obliged to protect us, Baby would whine and rest his massive head on my shoulder.

"Thank you for saving us. Good dog. Good dog," I said to Baby each time he "protected" us from a motley spate of irate mutts.

"Turn here," ordered June.

"Yes, I know," I complained, turning the cart a sharp right onto a badly maintained gravel road. Oh Lordy, was it *badly* maintained!

I hit a pothole, and June was almost thrown out of the cart. "Hold on!"

"This road is disgraceful," June spat out. Her eyes narrowed, and her face turned a hot shade of pink under her already heavily rouged cheeks. June was working herself up to chew nails and spit out barbwire. Gone was the cool, collected Lady Elsmere. This gal was all June Webster from Monkey's Eyebrow, Kentucky and fighting mad.

Oooh-whee, this was gonna be fun to watch! I suddenly felt much better about the world.

The road meandered into deep woods littered with abandoned washers, old tractor tires, rusty shells of cars, refrigerators, and other assorted metal trash. Scattered among the refuse were crude, hand-painted signs with messages like "PIGS LIVE HERE" or "WILL SHOOT YOU ON SIGHT" or "GIT OUT NOW AND YOU MIGHT LIVE!"

Charming, huh?

Rounding a bend, we came upon a freshly mowed meadow and saw a deputy's cruiser parked next to a shiny new Lexus. Beyond the cars was a cattle fence, behind which stood a little cottage that reminded me of a hobbit's den—cute, tidy, and perfect for one Rosamond Rose, a shy, retired, widowed librarian who took in stray animals and gave them a forever home. She had no kith nor kin to speak of, and her dearest friend was June's butler and heir Charles Dupuy, who also was an equally devoted animal lover and helped her out from time to time with vet bills and feed. Everyone called Rosamond "Rosie."

At the moment, Rosie was standing behind a red metal farm gate, frantically waving to us while talking on her phone. Her dogs were barking excitedly from inside her house and pawing at the windows.

I helped June out of the cart and told Baby to stay, so he straightaway jumped out and trotted after us.

June pushed through a knot of two deputies and one gnarled old man chuckling together.

The old man wiped the smile off his face when June stood squarely in front of him. "What are you doing, June? You are as welcome here as a breeze coming off an outhouse."

Rosie called out, "He locked me in, June. I can't get out. I'm on the phone with my lawyer right now."

I walked over to the fence where Rosie stood and yanked on the chain securing the gate to the post. "He's put a chain and lock on her gate."

June spat at the county deputies. "What are you two knuckleheads doing about this? Get your bolt cutters and set this woman free."

One of the deputies retorted, "He says she owes him back rent, and he needs two thousand dollars before he'll let her out."

"You two must have rocks rattling around in your skulls. Miss Rosie doesn't owe this man one red cent. She is on *her* property, and if you had checked, you would have found that this man has a Protection Order against him for harassing this sweet woman. He is not supposed to be anywhere near this property for two years. Did you bother to check?"

The two officers quickly glanced at each other and looked back at June with blank expressions.

"Now, I think locking a woman up infringes upon her right to come and go as she pleases. Kidnapping for starters. Violating the PO. Lying to law enforcement officers. I think Miss Rosie's lawyer will throw a couple more charges into the mix before he's done, like making a formal complaint to your boss. What was the deal? Gage would slip you both a couple hundred from the two thousand?"

Both deputies blinked and shifted their weight, looking down.

"Thought so. Now let this woman out."

Both ashen-faced officers backed away and scurried to their vehicle.

"What do you have to say for yourself, Gage Cagle?"

Gage inched closer to June until they were almost touching noses. "Who do you think you are, Miss High and Mighty, coming over here and sticking your nose where t'warn't wanted?"

Baby growled and tried to step between Gage and June. I hurried over and pulled him away only to have Baby look up at me and whimper.

June didn't flinch but stepped even closer. "You're a mighty small man, Gage. Not in body, but in mind and spirit."

"Don't get uppity with me, June. I remember your ma used to make your dresses out of feed sacks. You think you can ride in here and tell me what to do, let me tell you somethun'. Don't you act like you're better 'n me. I knew you as a scrawny brat crying for extra biscuits and gravy at my ma's table 'cause there t'warn't nothing to eat at your house."

June's back was up. "Let me tell you *somethum'*, Gage Cagle. Don't piss on my back and tell me it's raining. You've done nothing but torment Rosie ever since your daddy sold her this piece of property."

"She's got no business squatting on the family farm."

"Rosie's not *squatting* on your farm. She's living on *her* farm, and your daddy and mother granted her the right-of-way through your family farm in perpetuity. I should know. I was a witness to the reading of their will."

"A handwritten will not worth the piece of paper it's on."

"It was and still is legal in Kentucky. They loved Rosie, and that's what you can't stand. You're just making a fool out of yourself, you old fool. Now, you really are in trouble. You've broken the conditions of the PO."

One of the deputies walked over to June and Gage while the other one sheepishly walked past me and cut the chain, placing it in an evidence bag. "Sorry, ma'am," he muttered. "We were just having a little fun."

"Some fun," Rosie shot back. She pulled the gate open and stepped out. "Are you going to arrest him?" she yelled at the other officer.

The deputy pulled out a pair of cuffs and said, "Mr. Cagle, we've got orders to bring you in. The Jessamine County DA wants to talk to you. The call came in over our radio."

"You're going to cuff me, boy?"

"Sorry, sir. Standard procedure."

As the deputy pulled Gage away, he screamed, "I'm going to make you pay, Little Miss Rosebud! You mark my words. You're going to get your comeuppance too, Juneytooney! You're nothing but white trash dressed up in your better's clothes! My mother wasted her time on you. I remember. Don't think I don't!"

"Make sure you add terroristic threats to those charges," June yelled at the police.

I was so angry with Gage that I let loose of Baby's collar. Suddenly aware he was free, Baby bounded after Gage, sensing he was the object of our scorn.

Seeing Baby lope toward him, Gage broke free and jumped onto the car hood.

This only made June cackle with laughter.

Rosie and I chuckled too. It was too rich seeing Gage frightened of one of the most harmless dogs in the Bluegrass. What was Baby going to do? Lick him to death? The worst Baby might do is sit on him. Of course, having two hundred pounds of canine muscle resting on one's chest could be cause for alarm.

"Don't tinkle on yourself, Gage," June called out.

Watching the deputies pull Gage off the hood, June

murmured, "Being around that old fart is like eating potato salad left out on the Fourth of July."

"Uh-huh."

"Drinking water out of a toilet."

"Stop. I get the picture."

June smirked and called, "Baby, come!"

Of course, Baby minded instantly and ran over. *Why doesn't he obey me like that?*

Rosie hugged June. *She tried this with me, but I backed away. You know I don't like hugs. What's wrong with a friendly handshake?*

But Baby liked hugs and enjoyed the one Rosie gave him.

"Thank you both so much. I was scared to death!" exclaimed Rosie. "Gage has tried some scummy stuff over the years, but he never pulled a stunt like this. What if my house had caught on fire or one of the animals needed medical treatment?"

"Or *you* needed an ambulance?" I pointed out.

Rosie put her fingers to her lips. "Didn't think of that."

"It's over," June said.

"For now. I don't know why that man will not leave me alone. He's crazy, June. I'm afraid of him. He's getting more violent. I fear one day he's going to kill me. I really do."

I didn't naysay Rosie because I thought she was right. Gage Cagle had a grudge against Rosie, and men

killed women all the time in Kentucky while little was
done about it.

June asked, "You want to stay with me, Rosie?"

"Much obliged for the offer, June, but my animals
need me. I couldn't leave them."

"You could come over during the day with one of
my workers to feed them."

"No, no. I'm afraid Gage might come back and hurt
them. You know he's already poisoned some of my
dogs."

"Suit yourself then. Call me if you change your
mind."

"Will do, June, and kindly thank you again. Thank
you, Josiah." She bent over and petted Baby. "And you
too, Baby."

"Twarn't nothing," June said, mimicking Gage.

We all laughed, but as I helped June back into the
golf cart, I was uneasy.

Kentucky isn't called the "dark and bloody ground"
for nothing.

I knew in my bones Gage Cagle wasn't finished
with Rosie.

4

June was quiet on the ride home, seemingly lost in her thoughts about the past. I wondered if some of the spiteful things Gage said had dredged up painful memories.

I nudged her with my elbow. "June, you said you grew up in Monkey's Eyebrow. That's way down in western Kentucky. What were you doing hanging around the Cagle family in the Bluegrass?"

"I said I was from Monkey's Eyebrow, which I am, but my father went to work for Gage's daddy. It seemed like Daddy was always behind the eight ball, so he came to the Bluegrass to look for work. Mr. Cagle hired Daddy to manage his farm and handle paperwork for him."

"Paperwork?"

"Mr. Cagle was illiterate for the most part. Could sign his name and do his sums, but that's about it. Looking back, I would say he was most likely dyslexic. You know, got his letters mixed up. He was by no means stupid, but he needed help with the written word. Daddy made sure all the farm expenses, bills of sale, and receipts were properly filled out, signed, and recorded, making sure Mr. Cagle wasn't hornswoggled in any of his dealings."

"That's how you came to know Gage?"

"Uh-huh, yes. He's a few years younger than I."

"You want to tell me why Gage hates you so much?"

"My family was poor. Very poor. Gage's father gave us a house to live in as part of Daddy's stipend, but still, Daddy had back bills to pay so money was always short. Once in a while, we had to skip a meal, so I would wander down to the Cagle's home and look waifish until Mrs. Cagle would invite me to dinner. She was always good to me."

June's face broke out into a wide smile. "Ah, Mrs. Cagle. What a dear, sweet woman! She had always wanted a daughter and took an instant shine to me. She taught me table manners, how to converse in polite society, and things a rich man would expect of a wife. Don't smirk, Josiah. There was no such thing as Women's Lib then. The women's movement was decades in the future. The things she taught me came into use, especially when I married my second husband, Lord Elsmere, but she also pressed upon me to be kind—noblesse oblige and all that. What's the point of having a lot of money if you can't help folks?"

June grew quiet again and stared at the passing countryside until she shivered. "Did I tell you Mrs. Cagle bought me my first important dress? It was to my first Homecoming Dance."

"What about the feed sack dresses?"

"You're probably too young to remember, but back in the day, chicken feed came in lovely patterned cotton sacks. Women used to take the emptied sacks and make everything out of them from aprons to baby clothes to dresses. I still have two dresses Mother sewed for me."

"I take it that Mrs. Cagle never made dresses out of feed sacks."

"She never had to. The Cagle family was rich."

"I would like very much to see those dresses, June."

"I'll have Amelia get them out of storage then. They mean a lot to me. My mother was an excellent seamstress."

"Is the fact Mrs. Cagle took a shine to you the reason Gage doesn't like you?"

"That and the fact my fortunes took a turn upward, and his family's went downhill after his daddy died. Everybody used to address his daddy as 'Mr. Cagle', but Gage is just plain Gage to his peers. He resents it because he wants to be king of the hill."

"Perhaps that's why he dislikes Rosie so much. His parents doted on her and sold land to her."

"I think that's one reason, but I think there's more. I don't know what. He just doesn't want anyone on his property leading to Rosie's house."

"Do you know why?"

June shook her head. "Haven't a clue, but I'm sure whatever it is, it's got to do with some sort of illegal activity. Ever since I've known Gage, he's been mixed up in something dishonest. First, it was running moonshine to dry counties and holding underground card games, then selling cigarettes on the black market. Now, I'm not against drinking or taking a drag off a fag now and then, and the Lord knows I've been known to bet on a pony or two, but the way Gage goes about getting his jollies, people get hurt. He doesn't care whom he has to step over to make a fast buck. I've warned Rosie to sell and get out, but she won't listen to me. Gage is never going to leave her in peace. Never."

I skirted onto Tates Creek Road. In a matter of minutes, Lady Elsmere would be safely ensconced in the Big House, and I would be happily sitting in front of the TV at Matt's house.

I assumed Rose would be safe while Gage was in jail.

Or so we all thought!

5

I pulled up to the kitchen entrance at the back of the Big House. As I helped June out of the golf cart, I could hear Bess singing as she baked. Bess was a daughter of Charles, heir to June's fortune. I always refer to Charles as the butler. That's how he started with June, but he was now manager of her entire estate.

I sniffed the air. "Bess is making cinnamon rolls! Think I'll come in and sit a spell."

Most people would refer to Bess as a cook. She had neither formal training nor a degree from some fancy cooking school, but she was an artist. Give her four items, and she would give you a feast. People were forever trying to steal her away from June, but Bess knew on which side her bread was buttered, and happily for me, baking was her specialty. Hot cinnamon rolls and cold milk, here I come.

I almost pushed June out of the way trying to get inside until I remembered myself. I opened the door for June and cracked, "Age before beauty."

June swept past saying, "Pearls before swine."

I was chuckling when I followed her inside, and then I stopped. Frozen.

At the kitchen table gobbling down freshly baked, hot cinnamon rolls sat Asa and her sidekick, Boris *Whatshisface*.

Asa put down a glass of chilled milk and sang, "Hello Mommy Dearest. I'm home."

6

Bess laid out more plates, glasses, and teacups on the table alongside a pan of her delicious cinnamon rolls with a pitcher of milk and a pot of hot tea.

Boris immediately poured hot tea into a clear glass. That's the Eastern European way I am told.

June poured tea into a cup and then added milk. That's the aristocratic British way I am told.

I poured milk into a glass. That's the Josiah way and the *correct* beverage to drink with warm homemade cinnamon rolls.

"You seem surprised to see me, Mother."

"Well, Asa, I'm quite floored but very pleased."

"Are you? You don't look it."

I managed to grimace a smile. "Are you on a case since *Whatshisface* is with you?"

"His name is Boris as you very well know."

"Sorry, Boris," I apologized, handing him a napkin.

"No offense taken," replied Boris, wiping the crumbs from the side of his mouth with the back of his hand.

"I think you missed the crumbs caught in your pelt," I added, remarking on the man's remarkable chest hair sprouting from his shirt.

Asa gave Boris a disapproving glance. "Quit clowning for my boorish mother."

I turned to June and mockingly asked in a Southern drawl, "Am I boorish? I ask you."

June decided not to play and said, "Asa, I'm so glad you're here. Just in time for the Bluegrass Antique Ball."

"Sorry, Miss June, but I'm only here for a short while, then I fly out again."

"Of course," I sniggered.

"What does that mean, Mother?"

June sighed. "Girls, fight your battle somewhere else. I don't want to waste what little time I have left listening to you two bicker."

"Sorry, June."

"Me too, Miss June," replied Asa. She mouthed over June's head, "You started it."

I stuck out my tongue when June wasn't looking.

Asa said, "I'm just here for a few days. Can you put Boris and me up? I went to the Butterfly, but Mother has it rented out this weekend, and there's not enough room at Matt's cottage for all three of us."

"Four," I said, getting up and opening the screened kitchen door in response to frantic scratching.

Baby happily bounded in and went straight to Asa

for a sniff and a scratch behind the ear. He looked warily at Boris with his lone good eye, sniffed again, and decided Boris wasn't worth his interest. No food.

"What? No hello for me, you worthless canine?" asked Bess, feigning anger.

Baby whined as he thumped his thick tail against the bottom cabinets. It sounded like someone hammering nails.

"Bess, please give Baby something to eat before he demolishes the kitchen cabinets," demanded June, irritated at the commotion Baby was making.

Bess put slices of roast beef into a stainless steel bowl she kept for Baby and the mélange of other dogs Charles brought home. She ran fresh water in another bowl and put it beside Baby.

"Miss June, I'll clean up the kitchen later, but I've got to get off my feet. Dinner will be at eight as usual."

"The kitchen is your domain, Bess. Do as you will."

Bess turned to Asa. "I'll be expecting you two for dinner?"

"That depends on Miss June," Asa replied.

June snorted, "You know you can stay."

Asa smiled with relief. She didn't want to stay at Matt's cottage with me? What was up with that?

"I'm coming too," I chirped, inviting myself.

My next thought was to wonder whether Asa and Boris were going to stay in separate rooms, but I didn't have time to ponder. Amelia, another daughter from

34

the union of Charles and Josephine Dupuy, wandered into the kitchen.

"I heard you put that old curmudgeon in his place, Miss June."

"News travels fast in these parts."

"Rosie called and told me the entire shameful episode."

"I got in the last word," June replied, straightening her shoulders.

"A ball of righteous fire is how Rosie described you."

"And me?" I asked.

Amelia grinned, remarking, "She didn't mention you specifically, Josiah, but Rosie did say Baby was a big help, too. Did that old bag of wind really pee on himself?"

June scowled. "Does a lady say the word 'pee?'"

"I heard you say the word piss today, June," I replied. June could be such a hypocrite—unlike me.

Amelia, Asa, and Boris looked at June in astonishment.

June grinned. "I did, didn't I?" She chuckled. "Charm school rubs off when dealing with a no-good, worthless dog—no offense, Baby—but it felt so good. Well, enough of this jibber-jabber. I leave you all to your own devices. See everyone at dinner." June rose and allowed Amelia to escort her upstairs.

"I need a nap also," I announced, rising. "Coming, Asa?"

"I'm going to take a walk after I unpack. Boris, if you would be so kind, please take my bag to the blue bedroom overlooking the pool. It's right across from Lady Elsmere's room. You take the room down the hall overlooking the front driveway."

"Okay, Boss."

Ooh, that answered my question about the relationship between Asa and Boris. Strictly business.

It made me a little sad. Boris, when not clowning around, was good-looking, square jaw and all, smart, and reeked of male hormones that said, "Let's get it on." He didn't seem to be a psychopath and had a sense of humor, a job, and all his own teeth. What more could Asa want?

It was my fervent belief all young people should be in love. I had been terribly in love with Asa's father, Brannon, and was very happy for a good many years until our marriage fell apart.

I wanted that for Asa. Not the awful part when a relationship comes undone, but the good part, the love of a good man for my baby girl and a home to call her own. I realize not every woman needs or even wants that, but how long could Asa keep up what she was doing? Her job had to take a terrible toll on her body and psyche. But then again, I had to admit Asa was probably a thrill junkie.

My path was not her path. I needed to let Asa live her own life and not interfere.

Why was Asa here? She rarely dropped in for no reason.

Was it to interfere with my life?

7

Boris took the overnight bags upstairs, leaving Asa and me alone in the kitchen.

Baby, now sleeping stretched out in front of the door, didn't count.

I asked, "What's up, Buttercup?"

"Why haven't you returned my calls or texted me back?"

I replied, "Just been so darn busy. It got away from me. I hope you didn't come all this way to check on me. As you can see, I'm fine."

"I flew all the way from Paris to see you."

"How is France this time of year?"

"Mother, quit trying to deflect. I was worried. What's wrong?"

I stood up. "Nothing my child needs to worry about. I admit I may not be at my best, but I'm still the parent here, Asa."

"Let me help. You may be the parent, but sometimes you aren't exactly the grownup."

Ouch!

"You have helped me by showing up, but I'm very sorry if you expected to find me in a puddle on the floor."

"I thought you might be in the hospital."

"If that had happened, you would have been notified."

"Oh, you're impossible, Mother!"

"And you said you wanted to go for a walk. Go to the nursery barn. The foals are there, getting checkups from the vet."

I started to rouse Baby when Asa asked, "Why are you on kidney medication?"

I froze.

"I've asked before about it, and you always denied using it."

Swinging around, I asked, "Did Franklin rat me out?"

"I searched your room."

"You had no right."

"This from a woman who begged me to buy addictive pain medication off the streets and smuggle it home."

"I never asked you to do such a thing, but I thank you for it. I would not have made it after my fall without that medication."

"I could have gone to prison if caught, Mother."

"You did it on your own, but I was grateful. The

thought you could be arrested didn't cross my mind, Asa. I'm so sorry."

"I don't regret it, Mother. I will do it again if you're in need of such strong medication. I know how much pain you were in. I also know Kentucky is royally screwed up regarding pain medication."

"Is this what you're mad about?"

"I'm not mad."

"You could have fooled me."

"Something is going on with you, and you are not telling me."

"My darling girl, I know we don't see eye to eye on many things, but you don't need to look out for me. I'm fine. Yes, I'll admit since Matt has been gone, things have been a little rocky for me, but I'm finding my footing again, and I will be okay. Please don't worry about me. Live your life. Have fun. Catch bad guys. Have a romantic encounter with Mr. Boris *Whats-hisface*."

"And get sued for sexual harassment? You know he's my employee."

"I somehow don't think Boris would mind canoodling with you."

"Bad idea."

"I'm full of bad ideas. They are what makes life so enjoyable."

Asa sighed. "It's at times like this I wish I smoked crack or drank myself stupid or took candy away from small children or—"

I cut in, "I get the picture."

"You are so frustrating."

"I'm frustrating?"

"I can see I'm not getting anywhere with you, so I'm going to walk to the horse barns."

"Shaneika is training Comanche at the track here. You might run into her."

Asa wrapped her arm around mine as we stepped over Baby and went out the kitchen door. She held the door open for Baby. "Baby, come!"

Baby yawned and sleepily got up, leaving a hairy outline of his body. He had shed fur on the kitchen floor. Oh dear! Bess would have a fit.

I suggested, "Take my cart and take Baby with you. I'm going to clean this mess up. I can't leave the floor looking like this. Bess would skin me alive."

"Don't you dare steal all of those cinnamon rolls. I want some more."

"Me, steal?" I said, grinning. I was already wondering how many rolls I could stuff in my pocket.

My daughter knew me too well.

8

Lady Elsmere, Rosie, Asa, and I squeezed into the back of June's Bentley. Boris and Charles sat up front. Amelia followed in another car.

June was dressed in a 1960s satin pale green gown with a sequined full-length green paisley coat of the same material. She was wearing her emerald ring and necklace—worth a king's ransom. Her wrists sparkled with multiple emerald bracelets accented with diamonds along with Burmese ruby bracelets.

Rosie wore a yellow and pink knee-length gown with pointed high heels that matched, complemented by a single strand pearl necklace. She told us it had been her high school prom dress. I was amazed she could still get into it—or was I jealous? Maybe a little of both. Lord knows I've struggled with my weight.

Asa was poured into her strapless black velvet gown with a sweetheart neckline. Her dark hair was swept up into a French bun, held together with diamond and platinum hairpins June had loaned her.

I wore my usual Grecian blue chiffon Dior dress but with shoes this time instead of house slippers. My hair was styled and my makeup applied. We were a gaggle of good-looking gals for a night on the town, heading for the prestigious Bluegrass Antique Auction and Ball.

"Where's Miss Josephine? Isn't she coming?" I asked Charles concerning his wife.

"She's not up to it. She's still afraid she might fall, so I'm going stag," replied Charles, referring to his wife's recent fall in a horse barn. She had tripped over a rein from a bridle that had not been secured in the tack room.

"What am I?" June snarled. "Chopped liver?"

Asa chided June. "You know what he means. You're being ornery." Asa leaned forward and patted Charles on the shoulder. "Tell Miss Josephine we miss her and wish her a speedy recovery."

June waved her hand and barked, "Enough of this chitter-chatter."

I knew June had her eye on several eighteenth-century chairs made by a notable Kentucky furniture maker and was determined to get them by any means necessary. That's an overstatement, I'm sure, but she was bound and determined to get her way even though Asa was cautioning her.

"Miss June, it is rare that a signed piece of eighteenth-century furniture by a Kentucky cabinetmaker comes up for sale, let alone several chairs at once. I would be very cautious."

"I appreciate your concern, but these chairs are being sold by a reputable dealer."

Asa said, "Um, I deal with experts all the time and consistently find they're bamboozled by con artists more often than they would want you to know."

"June, would it hurt to have Asa check them out before you bid?" I asked.

"I think it is a good idea," Rosie chimed in.

June rattled her bracelets, capitulating. "If you insist."

Asa sat back. "Good. What are you going to do with those chairs anyway? You don't need them."

"That's not the point, Asa. Kentucky has a proud heritage, and I want to help preserve it. I'm going to donate them to a museum I'm thinking of opening in Lexington."

"This is the first I've heard of such a museum. Charles, did you know about this?" I butted in.

Charles talked over his shoulder. "Lady Elsmere has had this on her mind for some time."

Rosie asked, "What will be the name of this museum?"

"The Charles Dupuy Museum of Kentucky."

Charles slammed the brakes, causing all of us to jerk forward.

I put my arm out to safeguard June as I heard Amelia screech her car to a halt behind us.

Charles turned around in his seat. "No, you don't, June. If you do, my life won't be my own. I'll be pestered from dawn to dusk from folks wanting stuff in their attics to be appraised, and then they'll get mad when they're told their great grandma's sauerkraut crock ain't worth nothing. No siree, you put that museum in your own name."

June pursed her lips.

Charles started driving the car again, muttering under his breath, "The woman will be the death of me. She comes up with the craziest ideas."

As June seethed, Asa bit her lip to avoid smiling.

"Well, I never," June said. "You try to do something nice for someone, and they give you grief over it."

"Charles does have a point, June. I don't think he's ready to be thrust into the limelight like that yet, and he does have a lot on his plate right now," I said.

Charles was still learning how to manage June's estate since he was her heir. It involved taking management courses and meeting with her lawyers along with the day-to-day running of her properties. It was a massive undertaking.

Rosie looked embarrassed. Her chest flashed red, and I watched the color rise up her neck and onto her cheeks.

Trying to reassure her, I said, "It's okay, Rosie. They

fuss like this all the time. It's nothing. This disagreement will be forgotten in five minutes because they'll be arguing about something new."

"Oh," Rosie said to June. "I didn't know you and Charles were so close."

"He's my right hand. I don't know what I would do without Charles," June replied and then leaned forward to make sure Charles heard her. "Except he's a stubborn mule. Yes, you are, Charles. I see you eyeballin' me in the rearview mirror. You don't scare me none."

Asa broke out into peals of laughter.

Boris and I both joined her.

Even June broke into a smile. She loved jousting with Charles, and everyone knew he would come around to her way of thinking. Charles realized that when he did inherit June's estate, he would become a public figure in the Bluegrass. He just had to wrap his mind around the idea of a museum before he cottoned to it.

Our merriment for the night would soon end, though we didn't know it at the time.

9

Our little retinue made a splendid entrance to the Bluegrass Antique Auction and Ball, which had been a horse training facility before it was transformed into an auction house located on the north side of town. One could still smell the faint odor of horse sweat and manure after a heavy rain.

Asa, Rosie, and I entered first. Then Her Ladyship entered on the arms of both Charles and Boris. Talk about June being an attention hog.

Everyone stopped talking and turned around to gawk.

June smiled her royal smile, nodded, and said hello to friends as she entered. I swear some women even curtsied. They were small curtseys to be sure, but a curtsey is still a curtsey. Thank goodness they weren't doing the Texas Dip.

A Texas Dip is when a lady lowers her forehead to the floor by crossing her ankles, then bending her knees and sinking. As the woman's head nears the floor, she turns her head so she won't spoil her dress with lipstick. You'd have to be an acrobat to perform that curtsey.

After everyone said hello to June, they began milling about perusing items intended for the auction, including Asa who drifted away to evaluate the two chairs June intended to bid on.

I sauntered around talking to people I knew, glancing over occasionally to check on June.

Boris was standing behind her with his hands clasped in front of him, but I could see he was scanning the crowd.

Why had Asa ordered Boris to stand guard?

I looked for Charles, finally spotting him registering June so she could bid. Afterward, he ran into people he knew from the Animal Humane Society's Board, of which he was a member, and stopped to chat.

For some reason I was nervous, but I couldn't pinpoint why. I just had a sense the evening would not end well. You know, don't you, when you get a certain foreboding that something dark is nipping at your heels? You can't see it. You can't hear it, but you know it's near and closing in. That's the feeling I had.

Someone gently tapped me on the shoulder. I turned around to see Deliah Webster standing in front of me beaming. She was wearing a red '80s sequined dress with a neckline plunging down to her navel showing off her obvious asset—two of them, in fact. I guess the ample cleavage was to take one's mind off the extensive shoulder pads rising from either side of her lovely neck.

"Deliah, my, my, my. What a dress!"

"Thank you. I thought it was you, Josiah. I haven't seen you since the trial."

Deliah was referring to Peter Russell's trial for the murder of Madison Smythe. Deliah, Madison, and I had participated in an amateur theater group and were rehearsing *The Murder Trap* by Abigail Keam when the husband of one of the other players tried to murder his wife by putting ethylene glycol into the thermos she took to rehearsals. The only problem was he killed the wrong person, Madison, who was our lead actress. Deliah and I testified for the prosecution.

Deliah sniffed. "It's a shame our little drama group is no longer meeting."

"I think the murder cast a pall. Who can enjoy putting on a play when so many lives were ruined by Peter?"

"It's a shame he didn't get the death penalty."

I didn't want to talk about Peter, but said, "He did get life without parole."

"Did you hear about Ashley?" Ashley was a young man in our group who helped Peter—unwittingly, he says.

I shook my head.

"He got fifteen years. The jury rejected his story

ABIGAIL KEAM

that he didn't realize Peter was trying to murder his wife."

I didn't reply, as Madison Smythe's death was a terrible blow to many people, so I tried to change the subject. "Are you interested in antiques, Deliah?"

"I'm not. Asa told me to be here. I work for her now. Didn't you know?"

I lied. "Yes, of course, but what are you doing at this particular event?"

Deliah held up a camera. "I'm to take pictures of all items for sale and everyone who bids on them."

"Ah, I see."

"Do you? I don't see the purpose of it, but I do what I'm told because I'm making good money working for Asa, plus it's exciting, and I meet all sorts of interesting people."

"Did Asa instruct you to wear a low-cut dress?"

"The lower, the better, she said."

"Uh-huh."

"I'm supposed to be a distraction."

"And that you are, my dear."

"I just saw Asa give me the evil eye, so I'm off. You have a good night, Josiah."

"I'll do my best. Keep your chin up and chest forward, Deliah."

Deliah flashed her pearly whites before heading toward the open bar, snapping pictures along the way.

Thinking Deliah had a good idea about heading for

the bar, I decided to follow. On the way, I was detained by several people I knew, having to make small talk. *Hello. How are you? How are the children? Oh, your daughter quit college, is pregnant, and living with a drug addict. I see. Yes, I can understand why you are in therapy. Maybe your daughter should go with you. How's your mother? Oh, she died last month. So sorry. I'm doing great. Yes, let's do lunch sometime. Toodles.*

"You have such lovely friends, Josiah."

Recognizing the voice, I turned to meet the "she-dragon" as I uttered, "Agnes Bledsoe. Aren't you dead yet?"

Agnes smiled. "And give you the pleasure? I should say not."

Agnes is the ex-wife of Richard Pidgeon who was found dead in one of my beehives. Richard's second wife, Tellie, tried to frame me for the murder. I guess she didn't like me.

"I see you got a new rug," I said, referring to her short black haircut.

Agnes reached up and tugged on her bangs. "This is my hair. The cancer is in remission. So sorry to disappoint, but I'll be dancing on your grave, Josiah." Agnes didn't like me either.

"No doubt. I hope that's all you do on my grave."

"What are you doing here? You don't like antiques. You collect mid-century crap."

"How would you know?"

"I took a tour of the Butterfly. I had to see for myself what all the fuss was about."

"Thanks for letting me know. I'll have the house fumigated."

Agnes smiled sweetly at me. Was I losing my touch to irritate her?

"Why are you here, Agnes?"

"There's a sweet little sugar chest I've got my eye on."

"Do you know anything about those eighteenth-century comb-back writing chairs by Porter Clay?"

"I looked at them."

"And?"

"My interest lies in American neoclassical furniture 1800 to 1820."

"Agnes, those chairs were made in 1799, only a year earlier."

"So?"

"So, I know you collect very early American furniture. I remember seeing a Duncan Phyfe piece in your office."

"But only after 1800. Sorry, can't help you."

"Won't help, you mean."

"What is it you want to ask, Josiah?"

"Would you buy those chairs if you were interested?"

Agnes thought for a moment. "You're asking for your pal Lady Elsmere, aren't you?"

"Yes, she plans to bid on them."

"I'll give you a straight answer since Lady Elsmere is one of my clients."

That was news to me!

"I would steer clear of them."

"Why?"

"They look too crisp. You know that saying—*if it's too good to be true, it probably is.* Writing chairs would be one piece of furniture to have been heavily used for anything from writing a letter to stringing green beans. The chairs are worn where they are supposed to be, but I don't know. Something is off."

"Like a boy carving his initials into the wood with a new penknife he got for Christmas?"

"Exactly."

"That could explain the date 1799 and the initials P C carved under the seat drawer."

Agnes waved to someone behind me. "Look, I've got to go, but those initials were carved by an adult, not a child."

Suddenly, Agnes' eyes dilated as she looked past me. "Josiah, be cool now. Don't cause a scene. Ciao." She hurried off and greeted a man by kissing him on the cheek. He was good-looking and young—too young.

I watched Agnes and her fancy man before I lost interest. So, Agnes was officially a cougar. Good for her. Why should only old men have young dates? Not fair, is it?

Don't cause a scene? What could Agnes have meant?

There was a slight hush amongst the crowd as I turned to see Ellen Boudreaux. I had to admit she looked lovely holding onto the arm of her new beau.

Ellen was my late husband's mistress and bore him a child while he and I were still married. I'll not tire you with the gory details of my marriage's demise, but it was a mess. I lost my job as an art history professor and came close to losing the Butterfly and the farm due to Brannon's financial shenanigans.

Even though my husband's betrayal devastated me, I eventually made peace with it, but Asa hadn't. She could not forgive her father for leaving us destitute, and she hated Ellen for not letting her visit her half-brother.

Oh dear! Had she seen Ellen?

Out of the corner of my eye, I saw Asa spot Ellen and rise from her chair only to have June reach up and pull her back down. It was clear no one was going to disrupt the auction if June could help it.

Now I really needed a drink—a big stiff drink with lots of bourbon in it. A Kentucky Mule sounded fine and dandy. I made my way to the bar, hoping to get a drink and find a corner to hide in before someone else spied me and started talking to me. By the time I got there, my rotten demeanor was further marred by people stepping on my toes or drunkenly bumping into me. People were already three sheets to the wind, and the bidding hadn't even started. I'm sure the event organizers deliberately allowed the attendees to become well lubricated with alcohol before the bidding commenced.

I got my drink and was heading to a quiet corner when someone jostled my arm, causing me to spill my cocktail on the man in front of me. "Oh, I'm sorry."

The slight man turned around and smiled painfully, like a man grinning through a toothache.

I winced, noting the man was irritated but trying to be polite. "I really am so sorry."

Taking a handkerchief from his pocket, the man patted his coat sleeve. "No harm done. Don't give it a second thought." He looked up, scrutinizing me until recognition hit. "You're Mrs. Reynolds, Lady Elsmere's friend."

"Yes."

He extended his hand. "I am Eli Owsley, owner of the Owsley Antique Emporium in Cincinnati."

I shook his hand, pleased he wasn't a hugger. "How did you know who I am?"

"Lady Elsmere contacted me about certain items being auctioned tonight, so I made it my business to learn about her. Your name came up. You are her neighbor, no?"

"Yes, I live next door. Do you always vet potential customers, Mr. Owsley?"

"I consider it part of my customer service to know my customers and their preferences, Mrs. Reynolds."

"I see."

"I confess I have read about you and your sleuthing exploits in the paper. You recently testified in a murder trial, didn't you?"

"I'm sure you understand I'm not allowed to talk about my testimony, Mr. Owsley," I lied.

Mr. Owsley scanned my clothes and jewelry, sizing me up. I felt almost naked, but I doubted he was interested in me in a carnal way. Mr. Owsley had the faint smell of greed about him. "Are you going to bid tonight?"

"I'm here for the free champagne."

Mr. Owsley's mouth turned downward. Realizing I was of no use to him as a potential customer, his eyes slid past me. "I see Lady Elsmere beckoning. Please excuse me."

"Of course," I replied, stepping out of the way before he ran me over. I was feeling most foul. My drink had spilled, and I had been dismissed by a grasping little twerp as not even important enough for small talk. It didn't help when someone lightly goosed my bottom.

"Jumping Jehoshaphat!" I gasped, swirling around, ready to smack the man who dared touch me in such a familiar fashion.

Franklin stood there grinning like the Cheshire Cat. "Hello, Gorgeous," he said in a Brooklyn accent and gave me a big hug, which he knew I didn't like. What a stinker!

Behind him stood Hunter. Both of them were dressed in tuxedos with Hunter looking quite smart in a classic black tuxedo, while Franklin sported a powder blue, crushed velvet jacket with a ruffled white shirt.

I pushed Franklin away. "Which one of you mashers touched my derriere?"

Hunter stepped forward and kissed me on the cheek.

I caught a whiff of his cologne, which smelled divine on his clean-shaven cheek.

"I cannot tell a lie. It wasn't I," Hunter said, giving Franklin a little push. "Go away, baby brother. Three's a crowd."

"I can take a hint. Besides, I've spotted Asa. She will welcome me with open arms. Good Lord! She's turning one of those rickety old chairs upside down. I've got to see what she's up to."

Hunter pulled me over to a dark corner, wrapped his arms around my waist, and whispered in my ear, "You look so delectable tonight, I could eat you with a spoon."

"That sounds both thrilling and icky," I murmured, giggling like a schoolgirl before realizing I hadn't spoken to Hunter in several weeks.

I pulled away. "Hey, wait a moment. Where have you been?"

"Where have I been? You're the one not returning my phone calls or texts. I had to call Eunice to see what was going on. She said you were having a mid-life hissy fit, and I shouldn't take anything you said or did personally until you snapped out of it."

"You could have driven over to check on me."

"I was trying to get my life back on track so I could pay you the attention you deserve."

"Yeah. Right," I scoffed.

"No, really, Josiah. I think I have a buyer for the farm. It's not set in stone, but we are coming close to the figure I need. It could be a game changer for Franklin and myself."

"To whom are you selling?"

Hunter flinched.

"Oh, Lord, no! Not to a developer?"

"I have no choice. No one wants to buy a run-down plantation with a dilapidated antebellum house with leaking pipes and fifteen-foot ceilings. The heating bill alone can break the budget of a small city."

"There are people all over the world who would give their eyeteeth to own a property such as yours."

"Where are they? I haven't got so much as a nibble from people interested in raising horses or preserving the land."

"You haven't looked hard enough."

"You're not fair, Jo. I'm broke and running out of options before I have to declare bankruptcy." He pulled me closer and nuzzled his chin against my cheek, taking a deep whiff of my hair. "Please, Josiah, let's not fight. I came here to see you. Nothing else mattered but that I spend time with you tonight."

Like the sucker I am, I melted into a puddle. Was I being unfair? Probably. I had the same problem with my farm. I had been going under too but got a settlement from the city, which turned the fortunes of my farm around.

Hunter didn't have the luxury of a financial windfall. So, yeah, I was being a bit of a butthead. It was just so hard to see another piece of the beautiful Bluegrass destroyed forever for tacky McMansions. It made me want to cry.

"Once I sell the farm, I'm going to move in with Franklin in the city until I can find a suitable place of my own."

"What are you going to do with all your heirlooms and furniture?"

"Franklin and I will keep what we want. Then we're going to sell the rest at auction."

I sighed. "It looks as though you both have thought this through. I'm sorry for I know you love Wickliffe Manor."

"Let's not talk about it anymore. I'm here to have fun with my best gal. I want to look on the bright side of this tragedy. I will have money to give my lady whatever she desires."

I gave a faint smile. What I truly desired was for Wickliffe Manor to stay intact, but we don't always get what we want in life.

Gee, that's an understatement.

10

In an effort to forget the gloomy news, Hunter and I drank champagne and nibbled on some hor d'oeuvres, the remains of which Hunter deftly deposited in the base of a flower arrangement.

"The canapés are awful. They should have hired Eunice as the caterer," I said.

Hunter drank more champagne to get the unpleasant taste out of his mouth. "Stale. Very stale."

I nodded in agreement.

"Let's go see Lady Elsmere and save her from Franklin chewing her ear off."

I glanced over and saw June and Franklin engrossed in a gabfest. He had already managed to wrangle one of June's ruby and diamond bracelets off her wrist and was wearing it around one of his ankles. Did I mention he wasn't wearing socks? It was an interesting look to say the least.

Asa was sitting on the other side, trying to get June's attention. "Franklin, can I get a word in edgewise?"

Franklin sniffed. "If you must interrupt?"

"June, I looked at those Windsor chairs, and I would not bid on them."

"What's wrong?"

"Nothing obvious. They're in mint condition. The dovetail joints are how they should be. The wood smelled right and was worn where it should be. The legs are nicked where the heels of a gentleman's boots would have struck them."

"What's the problem?"

"I don't know, but my nose is twitching. There's something hinky about those two chairs. The auction catalog says they came from the same collection, but it would be very unusual for a household to have two. I've always found a house to have one writing chair. Why would they need two? It's like having two refrigerators in the kitchen."

"But some people do have two refrigerators in their kitchen. I do, and your mother does. These chairs were commissioned by Roald Jansen, a Norwegian who became rich by planting hemp near Cynthiana."

"That's a red flag for me. Why would a Norwegian immigrant commission English designed chairs?"

"English? I thought the Irish first designed Windsor chairs."

"Perhaps the Welsh, but that's not the point, Miss June. Chairs like these are heavily used. Typically, something is missing like a drawer or a spindle, and it's not unusual to see signs of repairs. Except for some nicks here and there, these chairs are almost perfect."

"Asa, you have not given me any real evidence of something being wrong. Just a feeling, you say. These chairs were very popular and functional as well. Jansen would have commissioned furniture that was in the style of the times to keep up with the 'Joneses.' He wanted to fit in with his rich friends, and what better way to boast about his fortune than to commission two of these chairs?"

"I have never seen a bill of sale for Windsor chairs made by Porter Clay. My nose is not wrong. Trust me. Please don't bid on them."

"Listen to her, June Tooney, because I want those chairs."

Everyone gasped except for Boris, who unclasped his hands and put one inside his tuxedo, ready to pull his gun out if necessary, while Asa positioned herself directly in front of Rosie.

Rosie reached up and clutched Asa's hand.

There stood Gage with a big old smile on his craggy face.

"How did you get out of jail, Gage?" June asked.

"The judge is an old friend of mine and very sympathetic to my case. He threw the Protection Order out, saying it should never have been issued in the first place."

Rose spoke up, "I'll go to the DA first thing in the morning."

"Tomorrow is Sunday. A lot can happen between now and Monday morning."

Boris asked, "Are you threatening this lady?"

Gage drew back, acting hurt and insulted. "Look, friends. I'm here to bid on some antiques. I wanted to let you know I'm willing to let bygones be bygones. I've decided not to sue for my unlawful arrest. Of course, it will be my right to shoot your dog, Josiah, if I see him on my property again, and the same goes for *any* dog I see on my property." Gage glared at Boris.

I stiffened. I was getting tired of people threatening Baby. It had been going on for years now. I wanted to punch Gage in the nose, but there were too many witnesses. Sometimes it's best not to say or do anything.

Hunter curled his hands into fists and shifted on the balls of his feet.

I pulled on his coat sleeve and gave a slight shake of my head. It was best we didn't interact with Gage, but instead act as witnesses when we went with Rosie to the DA on Monday.

Gage continued to bluster. "But then again, I might miss that hound of yours and hit you accidentally, Josiah—or maybe you, Rosebud."

Did Gage just threaten to kill Rosie and me?

Rosie hissed, "You stay away from me. I mean it, Gage. I've had enough of your bullying."

Gage ignored Rosie, turning his attention to June.

"Don't you start licking your gravy yet, June. I've got my eye on them chairs. Let the best man win."

"Or best woman," June replied.

"No contest then." Gage winked at June and nodded at the rest of us before sauntering over to a knot of his friends drinking on the patio.

"There's a man who brightens a room when he leaves it," Hunter remarked.

I was fuming. "He's got some gall."

Franklin looked confused. "What a hideous creature. What was he talking about? Was Baby on his property? Who is he? Tell me, someone."

No one answered because the auction was starting.

Charles ran over with June's paddle and helped her into a seat closer to the stage where they were rolling out the antiques.

The rest of us hung back because we were outclassed, out-moneyed, and out-finessed, except for Asa who snatched up a small Henry Faulkner painting for eighteen thousand dollars.

Jewelry, paintings, and dishware were auctioned first. Then came the furniture—mostly nineteenth-century pieces, but there were a few mid-century pieces, which I would have given my eyeteeth to own, but the days when I could throw money at beautiful but useless things had passed. Everything I purchased now had to be practical.

What a bore!

11

I *was* bored. Did I already admit to that?

"Quit fidgeting," Hunter said.

"The seats are too hard." We were sitting in the back, so no one saw me scooting this way or that, but several people turned around and gave us the eye.

"Mind your own beeswax," I advised, making a sour face.

Hunter scolded, "Nice."

"Let's get on with it," I groused. The auction pace was too slow for my taste. My leg was starting to ache, and I hadn't brought my silver wolf-head cane. I have no patience when my leg starts to throb. What I needed was a stiff drink. Heck with this sissy champagne. Bourbon with lots of ice. Maybe another Kentucky Mule made with bourbon, Ale8-One, and a twist of orange. Sounded delicious to me, but I was afraid to lumber over to the bar. I might miss June bidding on the chairs.

Looking around I tried to place everyone. Asa was

sitting next to Charles and June. Boris was standing near the bar striking his best James Bond pose. Rosie had met some friends and was sitting with them. Franklin was behind June and Asa, learning forward and constantly peppering Asa with questions until she turned around and smacked him on the head with her catalog.

Where was Gage? I scanned the crowd.

Gage was standing in the back on the right side, far away from us.

Skulking behind Gage was an odd-looking man wearing a rumpled gray suit and sporting a three-day beard. He held a rolled-up auction program very tightly in his hand. I guess I noticed him because of the intense expression on his face. He seemed agitated and nervous.

Hunter nudged me, and I turned to face the stage just as the eighteenth-century chairs were brought up.

The auctioneer announced, "We have a pair of matching eighteenth-century comb-back Windsor writing chairs with much of the original black paint intact from the estate of Roald Jansen, one of the first pioneers to settle the Bluegrass. The chairs are verified as not having been refinished since the black paint was applied. The chairs have continuously curved armrests and a sack back with two quill drawers. There are no repairs or breaks in the wood. The scooped saddle-shaped seat is made from walnut as well as both removable quill drawers, which have their original locks but no keys. All the spindles are intact as well and are made from hickory.

The armrest drawer is scratched underneath with the date 1799 and the initials PC. We believe that the initials PC refer to Porter Clay, brother to Senator Henry Clay.

We know Porter Clay returned to Lexington from Manhattan in 1799 as there is another bill of sale for bed frames from Mr. Jansen's estate that is plainly signed by Porter Clay of the same year. The signature on the bill of sale has been authenticated as Porter Clay's. We think the chairs are some of the earliest examples of Kentucky furniture and of great historical value. Included in your program is the complete provenance of the chairs. May we start the bidding at two thousand for the pair?"

June held up her paddle which had a number assigned to it.

"We have a bid of two thousand. Do we have a bid at three thousand?"

A woman sitting across the aisle from June held up her fan. I recognized her from June's parties as an antique dealer from Louisville. She had been a heavy buyer during the evening.

"Thank you, Madame. Do we have a bid at four thousand?"

June threw up her paddle again.

"Thank you, Lady Elsmere. The bidding now stands at four thousand. Do I have five thousand?"

The antique dealer held up her paddle and shot June a dirty look.

June held up her paddle again and barked, "You might as well quit bidding, Mamie. Those chairs are mine. Six thousand."

The audience gasped.

I sat up in my chair, taking notice. The evening had finally become interesting. Thank the Lord.

Asa leaned over and whispered to June. What was she saying?

The auctioneer wiped his glasses with his polka dot handkerchief. He asked Mamie, the Louisville antique dealer, "Madame, the bidding now stands at six thousand. Do you wish to bid at seven?"

Mamie shook her head. Being a good sport, she threw a kiss to June.

The auctioneer raised his gavel. "Going once. Twice."

"Ten thousand," a voice boomed from the back of the room.

Everyone turned in their seats.

"Sir, are you bidding ten thousand dollars?" asked the auctioneer, trying to make out who had bid in the audience.

"Who's bidding against me?" June demanded. She stood as Charles tried to calm her.

"I am, June."

I groaned.

It was Gage, standing in the back of the room with his homies.

June's eyes narrowed. "Eleven thousand!"

"Twelve thousand!" shouted Gage.

"We can go all night, you old buzzard. I want those chairs."

"So do I, but you don't have to be so personal, June. After all, this is for charity. Right?"

The auctioneer picked up his gavel, his squinty little eyes bright with anticipation. "Going once."

June snapped back, "Thirteen thousand."

"Fifteen."

The crowd murmured.

Excitedly, Hunter jumped to his feet, as did several others in the audience.

Enraged, June called out, "Twenty!"

Asa was frantically whispering to June, but June was having none of it. Asa turned and looked helplessly at me. I knew she had been advising June to quit bidding.

"Thirty."

"Forty!" June countered.

"Fifty!" Gage shouted smugly.

"Sixty!"

"Seventy-five thousand dollars!" Gage cried out.

Lady Elsmere, aka June Webster from Monkey's Eyebrow, grinned and said, "Too rich for my blood. You win, Gage. Congratulations."

"Madame, have you stopped bidding?" asked the auctioneer.

"Yes."

"Sir, your last bid was seventy-five thousand dollars."

Someone from the crowd yelled, "What's the matter, Gage? You look a little pale."

People twittered.

I had to admit the bidding war over those chairs was the high point of the night so far. My blood was up like everyone else's, and Gage did look like a deer caught in a headlight. His color was off, and he weaved a bit on his feet before he steadied himself by grabbing the back of the chair in front of him.

The auctioneer ordered, "Quiet. Quiet. The bid stands at seventy-five thousand dollars. Are there any other bids?" The auctioneer scanned the room, which had now become deathly quiet. "Going once. Twice," he paused, "three times." He banged his gavel. "Sold for seventy-five thousand dollars. Congratulations, Mr. Cagle."

Everyone clapped while many raced over to shake Gage's hand.

The auctioneer announced, "This concludes the auction portion of our evening. Y'all are invited to the ball. For those of you who purchased items, my staff will assist you. Please see them before you proceed to the dance area. Thank you."

In other words, pay before you play.

12

Hunter helped me out of my chair. Oh, great, my right leg was asleep.

"I didn't know Gage Cagle is a collector. Those chairs are not worth seventy-five thousand. Not even close."

"Nicely put, Hunter," Asa said, coming up to us. "If they were made by Porter Clay, they would have some historical significance, but not seventy-five thousand dollars' worth. If I were Gage Cagle, I would have the insignia tested."

"You can test for that?" I asked.

"Yes," she said, signaling to Boris.

He immediately trotted over.

"I'm going to the dance. Are you two coming?" Asa asked.

I looked at Hunter.

He wrapped my arm around him as we followed Asa and Boris into the ballroom.

Spying June sitting at a table with ladies of her own

age, I pulled Hunter along toward her table.

She looked at me with eyes twinkling like the diamonds she was wearing.

I bent over and asked very softly, "Did you set Gage up?"

June turned away from her friends so they could not hear her answer. "I knew as soon as Gage said he wanted those chairs, something was wrong, so I turned the tables on him, or should I say chairs. I knew I'd get him. Gage was always a lousy poker player."

"Do you think he did it to get back at you for interfering with Rosie?"

June shrugged. "Makes no never mind to me, but if that odious man thought he could take advantage of me, he's certainly learned his lesson, don't you think?"

"Seventy-five thousand dollars' worth."

June threw back her head and crowed, sounding like a rooster relishing a juicy bug before she swirled around in her seat to join her friends.

Hunter escorted me to a table where Charles and Rosie sat. Charles was eating, and Rosie was nervously fiddling with an empty champagne glass.

Hunter asked, "Rosie, can I get you anything from the buffet?"

"No, thank you."

"Charles?"

Charles shook his head while slathering cream cheese on smoked salmon. "No, Hunter. I'm fine. Thanks."

"Josiah?"

"As long as you're offering, load a plate up for me. I'm starving."

"I'm off."

I watched Hunter weave through the dance floor, only to be sidetracked by a woman he knew. They chatted while dancing couples zigzagged and bobbed around them. I saw Hunter give the woman his card before excusing himself. When I turned to ask Rosie if she knew the woman, she was gone.

"Charles, where did Rosie go?"

Charles looked up from his plate and scanned the room. "I didn't notice her leaving. She probably went to the ladies' room. You want me to look for her?"

"No. You're probably right. She's in the powder room or she's visiting at another table."

"What's the problem?" Hunter asked as he placed a plate laden with food in front of me. Franklin brought up the rear with drinks.

"Nothing. Rosie left, and I don't see her."

Franklin sat down beside me, pinching food from my plate. "She probably has an illicit romantic interlude somewhere."

"I wish you were having an illicit romantic interlude somewhere." I moved my plate out of Franklin's reach.

He immediately snatched goodies from Hunter's plate.

Irritated, Hunter said, "Franklin, get your own food."

"Don't I get a reward for carrying your drinks?"

Charles wiped his mouth with a heavily starched linen napkin before saying, "Franklin, don't forget to return Lady Elsmere's bracelet before we leave."

"What bracelet?"

"The one you're wearing on your ankle."

Franklin glanced down and looked back up at us with his best how-did-that-get-there expression.

Hunter nudged Franklin. "Give it to Charles now. He's responsible for all of June's jewels. You don't want the insurance company to cancel June's policy."

Franklin argued, "They wouldn't cancel because I'm wearing a bracelet."

"They might," Asa said, sitting down, "if your name is not on the policy entitling you to wear her jewels. They might renege if you were responsible for losing the bracelet. It's a clause in many policies as a way to escape paying if something is stolen. They certainly would run a background check on you. You've had your run-in with the law, Franklin. You're not in the market for more, buddy."

Franklin gulped and quickly took off the "bangle", handing it to Charles who slipped it in his inside coat pocket.

Boris wandered over to the table with several tall drinks in his hands.

"Vodka?" I asked.

"Water."

I gave Boris a look that questioned his honesty.

He smirked while handing Asa one of the glasses.

I think Boris liked teasing me.

Asa said, "This has been some night. I'm relieved June quit bidding on those chairs."

I inquired, "What is their real worth?"

"If the documentation is correct, perhaps nine thousand apiece at an important antique auction in New York or Boston with serious collectors attending."

Hunter whistled. "Wow, and your neighbor paid seventy-five thousand."

I fumed, "Gage is no neighbor of mine."

Asa nudged me. "Look over there."

I turned to where Asa indicated and saw Gage in a heated discussion with two men. One was Eli Owsley, who was jabbing Gage in the chest with his finger. Beside him stood the peculiar man in the rumpled suit slapping his program against the palm of his hand. If I read humans well, and I do, I would say those two men were quite angry with Gage.

Why would Eli Owsley be irate with Gage who just purchased his chairs for seventy-five thousand dollars? Especially since he would be getting a fat commission. And who was the elf with the rumpled suit?

Asa motioned to Deliah and pointed to the three men.

Deliah nodded and sauntered over to them. "Gentlemen, smile," she said.

The three men looked up just as Deliah snapped a shot.

The man in the shabby suit stepped forward, making an aggressive move toward Deliah, but was pulled back by Eli Owsley. All three men quickly moved outside into the garden.

Deliah glanced at Asa before moving to the other side of the ballroom.

Asa muttered, "That was odd behavior."

"Yes, wasn't it," Hunter drawled. "The only thing I can think to elicit such a response is that Gage just informed the antique owner that he doesn't have the money."

"I wonder who the other man is."

"Doesn't matter," said Hunter, sweeping me out of my chair. "We're here to have fun. Let's dance."

Hunter hustled me over to the dance floor before I could protest. While doing the foxtrot, I scanned for the three men over Hunter's shoulder. I didn't see them, but spotted Asa making the rounds chatting people up. I knew she was probing for information.

Ah, like mother like daughter. Nosey.

13

When tango music started, I begged off and sat down in the nearest chair.

Hunter disappeared into the crowd and brought back two plates of various desserts. I was in chocolate heaven, but before I could shove some deliciousness into my piehole, Charles tracked me down.

"Miss June is tired and wishes to leave."

"I'll take Josiah home, Charles."

"What about Miss Asa and *Whatshisface?*"

I surveyed the room. "I'm sure Asa wants to stay, but Rosie probably will want to go home."

"I haven't seen her for a while."

"I haven't either, Charles. Let me check the powder room."

"That would be nice. I'm getting a little sleepy-eyed myself."

Reluctantly leaving my edible delights behind, I ventured to the ladies' lounge, calling out Rosie's name.

No reply. I asked the ladies washing their hands if

they had seen Rosie, but they replied, "no."

"Maybe she's outside having a smoke," one of them suggested.

Rosie didn't smoke, but I thanked them and hurried over to the patio garden where several gentlemen were puffing on their cigars.

"Have any of you seen Rosamond Rose?"

They either shook their heads or muttered, "No, Josiah."

"If you see her, please direct her to Lady Elsmere's table. Her Ladyship is wanting to go home, and Miss Rose came with her."

"Will do."

"No problem."

"She might have gone back into the auction room to get away from Gage," one of them suggested.

Everyone knew of Gage bullying Rosie.

I asked, "Has he been bothering Miss Rosie tonight?"

"Didn't see anything, but Rosie has seemed skittish all night," the man replied.

"I'll check there. Thanks, fellows," I replied, trying not to show I was miffed when none of them offered to check for me. My leg was killing me, and I wished I had asked Hunter to look for Rosie, but I proceeded to the auction room.

It was empty.

Drats!

Where was that woman?

Knowing Asa and Boris were on the dance floor, I decided to recruit them in my search for Rosie. As I turned to leave the room, I heard a loud thump behind the stage.

"Hello? Rosie, is that you? Hello?"

Hearing a muffled whimper, I hurried up the stage steps and pushed aside the thick curtain that separated the stage from the back room where the antiques were stored, waiting to be carted off by their new owners.

I saw a flash of yellow behind an armoire and said, "Rosie, I've been looking for you all over," while making my way to her around some heavy furniture. "June wants to leave, honey."

She turned to face me. Her beautiful yellow dress was smeared with blood, and she was clutching a knife in her hand.

"Oh, my God! Are you hurt?" I asked, rushing over to her.

It was then I saw Gage Cagle lying on the floor. I pushed Rosie out of the way and bent over to check for a pulse.

"He's still alive. Call an ambulance. ROSIE! GET HELP!"

Rosie gave a terrified wail before she dropped the knife and fled.

I grabbed some packing material lying on the floor and tried to staunch the bleeding, but blood was everywhere. "HELP! SOMEONE HELP ME! HELP!"

I screamed for a long time before help came.

It was Agnes Bledsoe who finally heard me.

14

I was wearing an orange paper jumpsuit, fearing that if I moved suddenly, the paper would tear. Where would I be then? I guess begging for some tape.

A plainclothes detective walked into the room holding a file and shut the door.

"Where is Detective Kelly?"

The man replied, "My name is Detective Norbet Drake. Can you answer some questions for me?" He eased into a chair.

"Are you the lead detective?"

"I am."

"What happened to Detective Kelly?"

Drake ignored my question. "You are Josiah Louise Reynolds?"

"I am."

Drake leaned back in his chair. "Are you the same Josiah Reynolds I read about in the newspaper all the time? You like solving murders?"

"No one likes murder cases because murder is a

nasty business, but I have helped solve several cases by working with the police."

Drake perused the file he was holding. "More than just several. According to your record, Josiah, you have stumbled over twelve murdered bodies in a relatively short time."

"So, Gage is dead."

"Bled out before the ambulance got there. Arrived at the hospital DOA."

"I didn't think he was going to make it."

"Why is that?"

"There was so much blood. I couldn't hold back the flow."

"Can you tell me what happened? Did he attack you and you stabbed him in self-defense?"

"What? You think I stabbed him?" I drew back in my chair astonished.

"If you confess, the DA can give you a plea deal."

I jumped up. Riiippp! Great! I tore the backside of my paper jumpsuit, and now my bare fanny was hanging out. "You got this all wrong. I didn't do anything to that man but try to help him."

"Please sit down, Josiah." Drake studied the police report. "You were discovered with Gage Cagle, covered in his blood."

"Look, Norbet."

"It's Detective Drake."

"Then it's Mrs. Reynolds. I had to lean over him to

staunch the bleeding. Of course, I got his blood on my hands and my dress. It doesn't mean I killed him. I found Gage prostrate on the floor, already injured."

The door to the interrogation room burst open and in stormed Shaneika Mary Todd—my hero and my lawyer. She gave Drake a menacing look. "Don't say another word, Josiah."

"You're interrupting my interrogation, Shaneika."

"Ah, blow it out you know where," Shaneika said. "Is my client under arrest?"

"No."

"Then I'm calling a halt to your questions, and my client is leaving with me. If at any time you wish to question Mrs. Reynolds again, you will have to do it with me present. In other words, this dame has law-yered up."

Shaneika tossed a bag at me, glimpsing my backside. "I brought some clothes for you, and not a moment too soon."

"There's a bathroom down the hall where you can change," Drake said, picking up his file. "Make sure your client doesn't leave town."

"Don't let the door hit you on the way out," Shaneika said.

As soon as Drake closed the door, Shaneika turned her ire on me. "Haven't I told you not to talk to cops without a lawyer present?"

"Drake thinks I killed Gage Cagle."

"No, he doesn't. He's just trying to rattle you."

"He did a good job."

"Let's get out of here so we can talk. Get dressed first. I see that it must be a little drafty for you."

Grinning, I made sure those looking through the two-way mirror got a good view of my "twin assets" while leaving the room.

15

Shaneika, Asa, and I settled into a booth near the back of Al's Bar.

The clack of billiard balls striking one another masked our conversation.

We quickly gave our orders to the waitress, who yelled, "Two cheese and drag 'em through the garden." After she lumbered back to the kitchen, we got back to the business of talking, whispering quietly.

"You're going to have to tell the police what you saw or you could be charged with hampering an investigation," Shaneika said.

"Do you think the police are trying to pin the murder on me?"

"No. Other attendees at the ball have told the police they witnessed Rosamond Rose running away with blood on her dress."

"Where is Rosie now?"

"I don't know."

Asa and I glanced at each other. We both had the

sneaky suspicion Shaneika was lying.

"Did you touch the knife, Josiah?"

"I don't think so, but there is a possibility I pushed it out of the way when I was trying to find something to press on the wound."

"Mom, can you tell us what happened with as much detail as possible?"

"Charles said June wanted to leave. I told him that I wanted to stay and Hunter would take me home. I also stated you probably wanted to stay, too. I offered to look for Rosie as I thought she might be in the ladies' room, but she wasn't there. I asked around, and everyone said they hadn't seen her. I went out onto the patio where several men were smoking cigars. They said they hadn't seen her, but suggested I look in the auction room."

"Let me stop you. I will need the names of those ladies and gents you talked with concerning Ms. Rose."

"No problem."

Shaneika shoved her yellow legal pad at me.

I quickly wrote down the names.

Shaneika grabbed the pad. "Did you at any time follow Gage into the auction docking area behind the stage?"

"No."

"Let me ask you again. Did you at any time follow Gage into any part of the facility?"

"No. I did not. I was looking for Rosie. Gage was

the last person I wanted to see. Why do you ask?"

"Because a witness has stepped forward saying you followed Gage into the auction room."

"I did not at any time follow Gage anywhere. I was looking for Rosie. I had no idea that Gage was behind the stage. Who said I followed him?"

"Let's move on. What happened next?"

"I want to know who accused me."

Asa gently touched my arm. "Mom, answer the question."

My stomach started to rumble, and the taste of those awful canapés rose in my throat. Talk about heartburn. "I went into the auction room where I heard a noise."

"Did you hear a cry?"

"It could have been a cry, but I remember it more like a thump."

"Would you characterize the thump as a body falling onto the floor?"

"Shaneika, it could have been. I really don't know. I heard a noise. It alarmed me."

"Why?"

"I don't know. It was a noise that didn't belong."

"Go on."

"I ran up the steps to the stage and went behind the curtain."

"What did you see?"

"I saw Rosie."

"You saw Ms. Rose's face?"

"Not exactly. I saw her dress. I mean, I saw a yellow flash from behind some furniture."

"You saw the color yellow?"

"Yeah, but I knew it was Rosie because of the yellow. It was a distinctive color."

"Was she sitting or standing up?"

"Standing."

"Then what happened?"

"I went around some furniture to where she stood, saying something like 'June wants to go home.' I was trying to let Rosie know her ride was leaving."

"Then what happened?"

"Rosie turned around. There was blood all over the front of her dress, and she was holding a knife. She seemed frozen at first, as if in a daze, before she said, 'I didn't do this.'"

"Okay," Shaneika said, furiously taking notes.

"That's when I saw Gage on the floor and rushed over to him. He was still alive, and I yelled at Rosie to get help."

"You said you passed by her. Did you push her out of the way or have any contact with her person at all?"

"To tell the truth, I don't remember. It happened so fast."

Shaneika looked up from her legal pad. "You told Ms. Rose to go for help. What happened?"

"I gathered packing material from the floor to use

as a compress on Gage's wound. I looked up and saw Rosie fleeing."

"What made you think Ms. Rose was running away? You did tell her to go for help."

"Because she was going in the wrong direction. She went through an exit door on the right, which leads out to the parking lot."

"Okay. Go on."

"I kept putting pressure on Gage's wounds and yelled for help until someone found me."

"Who found you?"

"Agnes Bledsoe."

Shaneika smirked. "Your good friend, Agnes Bledsoe?"

"Yeah, isn't that crazy!"

"The blood on Ms. Rose's dress—was it smeared or splattered?"

I had to think for a moment. "Smeared."

"Do you believe Ms. Rose stabbed Gage Cagle?"

"If a man ever needed killing, it was he."

"That's not what I asked."

"I don't know, Shaneika. I didn't see anyone else."

"Do you think Ms. Rose has the capacity to kill?"

"It is not in Rosie's nature, but anyone can kill if pushed hard enough. Gage had been brutal with her for years."

"Give me some examples."

"He poisoned two of her dogs, cut her waterline

several times, put three-penny nails on the road to puncture her car tires, called her place of employment and told her supervisors that she was a drug addict and selling to teenagers."

Shaneika said, "Wow. I think I might be tempted to kill someone if they did that to me."

"Mom, didn't he shoot into her house one time?"

"Almost got her, too. The bullet buzzed right by her head, but Rosie couldn't prove it was Gage."

"Why didn't the police stop the harassment?"

"His family has been in Jessamine County since the first settlers came. They have a lot of influence in the county."

"I get it."

"After years of trying, Rosie did get a lady DA who was sympathetic to her case and took it to court. A Protective Order was put on Gage, stating that he was not allowed any contact with Rosie, but you saw how that turned out. He ignored the PO, got hauled back into court, and a judge who knew his family threw the PO out."

"Did Gage threaten Rosie at the auction?"

Asa said, "Yes, he threatened to kill Mother and Rosie."

"How so?"

Asa replied, "Hunter Wickliffe, Mom, Rosie, Lady Elsmere, and I were talking when Gage approached us and bragged he was going to bid on the Windsor chairs.

Then he started ranting about shooting Mother's dog if Baby, or any dog for that matter, came back on his property, and how he might miss, accidentally striking Rosie or Mom. It was bizarre."

I noticed Asa didn't mention that Boris was a witness as well.

"Unfortunately, his threats give both Ms. Rose and Josiah a motive for murder."

I took a sip of water, not knowing how to respond. I knew Shaneika was right.

Shaneika continued, "You say he killed two of Ms. Rose's dogs, and he threatened to kill Baby. Did Gage Cagle fear dogs?"

"June told me he feared big dogs," I answered.

"Did you see any evidence of that?"

"Uh-huh."

Shaneika looked up from her notes.

"June and I rushed over to Rosie's place when Gage chained her farm gate shut. Baby chased Gage onto the hood of a police car, and Gage soiled himself."

"That's not good."

"You know Baby wouldn't have hurt him."

"Baby weighs two hundred pounds. He's all muscle and built like a small tank. I would jump on a car if he rushed me."

"Mastiffs don't usually bite."

"But Baby can easily knock a grown man to the ground, causing a great deal of damage, especially to an older person. You need to keep closer control over him."

I don't like it when anyone criticizes my precious Baby, but I kept my mouth shut.

Asa asked, "What's your advice at this point, Shaneika?"

"I think you both should go home and get some rest. I will call the police to set up an appointment. Josiah, you will answer their questions to the best of your ability. After that, you are to have no contact with them. Everything has to go through me."

"Am I in trouble?"

"I don't think Detective Drake is seriously considering the witness' claim that you followed Gage, but I'll sound him out. We could have finished the interview this evening, but I'm not in the habit of having a client give a formal statement to the police with her derriere hanging out of her pants. It puts my client on the defensive."

I chuckled. "Does it ever!"

"When this is all over, you might want to give Agnes Bledsoe a call."

"Whatever for?"

"She vouched for you. Agnes told the police that you were struggling to save Gage's life when she found you. And that you were many things, most of them irritating, but if you were going to murder someone, you would do it in such a manner as not to get caught."

"That's so sweet. I think I'm tearing up."

"Can you tell us who put the whammy on Mom?"

"I bet it was Ellen Boudreaux," I said. "She hates my guts."

"I don't know, but again, I'll find out what's going on. Just one more thing before you go. Could you identify the knife if you had to?"

I shook my head. "I saw something sharp and covered with blood. Other than that, I couldn't tell you anything about the knife."

"That's interesting."

"Why?" Asa asked.

"Because Mr. Cagle wasn't stabbed with a knife."

I was flabbergasted. "What was it then?"

Shaneika put her pad and pen in her briefcase, saluted, and walked out of the bar, passing our waitress who was delivering two plates of food to our table.

I turned to Asa, who was biting into a cheeseburger. "I hate it when she does that."

Asa bobbed her head in agreement while wiping ketchup off her mouth with a paper napkin.

It bothered me that Shaneika knew something I didn't. In fact, it kept me up all night wondering.

What had Rosie been holding?

And where was she?

16

It was one o'clock in the morning when Asa directed Boris to park the black SUV off the side of the road. If anyone should stop and ask what he was doing, Boris had instructions to say that he had pulled over to make a call.

The full moon was bright, so Asa didn't need a flashlight to climb over the dry limestone walls criss-crossing the landscape. She was able to wind her way past curious bovine raising their heads to watch a human trotting through their pasture.

Asa didn't worry about stumbling upon horses because most farms brought them in at night, which was good because encountering a startled stallion would be dangerous.

It was over a mile to the building complex near the Kentucky Horse Park where the antique auction had taken place. Sprinting over the land, Asa could hear the distant yips of dogs alerted to an interloper.

The barking caused one sleepy person to turn on

her outdoor lights and peek out from behind her curtain before stepping out onto the porch, forcing Asa to hide behind a massive old-growth, bur oak tree. The lady scanned the pasture behind her house, and satisfied all was well, praised the dog for protecting the homestead and went back inside, turning off the lights.

Asa doubled down and ran even faster.

At last, she reached the compound, which sat off the road, easily scaling the twelve-foot-high chain link fence surrounding it and landing cat-like on the soft earth. The outbuildings of the old Thoroughbred training center provided needed cover, enabling Asa to quickly approach the main building.

Thank goodness she had the forethought to have Deliah surreptitiously photograph the keypad for the security system, which still operated from a telephone landline, when she photographed the rest of the building. From Deliah's pictures, Asa was able to memorize the layout of the compound.

Giving the place a quick perusal, Asa made her way to the back of the building. Disconnecting the security system was child's play. Taking a small black case from her pocket, she extracted several small tools and unlocked the back door. It creaked ever so slightly as she opened it just enough to squeeze through before slowly easing it shut behind her.

She needed a light. Reaching up, she switched on a headlamp attached to her mask, quickly making her way through the mass of furniture in the storage area behind the auction stage. It took several minutes to find the two Porter Clay comb-back Windsor chairs.

She breathed a sigh of relief.

Settling gently into one of the chairs, she removed the top quill drawer. With quiet proficiency, Asa extracted the screws holding the lock in place. Laying them on a white cloth she had brought with her, she used her state-of-the-art phone to photograph the screws from different angles and took close-ups.

Pulling back the cuff of her black sleeve, Asa peeked at her luminous watch. Time was running out. She hurriedly took more pictures of the drawer and the chair.

As she slid the phone into a pocket, she heard a door slam in the distance. She immediately extinguished her light and hunkered down.

The night watchman was making his rounds earlier than usual. Now would be a good time to leave, but the lock had to be screwed back and the drawer replaced in its chamber. She would have to accomplish this in the dark.

Taking off her gloves, she gingerly felt around for the drawer, and once she found it, she lowered it toward herself. So far, so good.

She felt inside the drawer, finding the lock. Holding her breath, she reached up, carefully searching for the screws. Finding one, Asa pressed the screw into her index finger, hoping the moisture on her skin would hold the metal until she could drop the screw into the drawer.

It worked!

Using the same procedure, she lowered two more screws into the drawer.

The door to the auction room opened!

Asa froze.

The room was suddenly bathed in fluorescent light from the guard turning on the lights.

Asa blinked and tried to adjust her eyes quickly. She needed a place to hide or the guard would find her. Oh boy, would she have a hard time explaining her presence. She would be arrested for breaking and entering for sure.

Putting a hand over her eyes, Asa spotted a large armoire. She crawled to the armoire and squeezed inside, clutching the quill drawer to her chest.

Oh no!

She had forgotten the white cloth and the last screw! There was nothing she could do about that now as the guard was climbing the stage steps.

Asa left the armoire door open just a tad to observe him make his rounds. If he discovered the white cloth and the missing quill drawer, she would have to create a diversion, allowing her to escape and make her way back to the SUV before the police came. That plan was iffy.

Or she could sneak up and hit the guard on the back of the head, knocking him unconscious.

Either scenario caused concern and had its drawbacks.

The guard pushed aside the thick curtain and wandered to the storage area. Asa could see him clearly now. He was a slightly-built older gentleman, probably a retiree who needed to keep busy.

Asa watched him pick up Waterford goblets from a dining table and examine the tags with the winning auction bids and names of the new owners. The guard shook his head at the prices before giving a sharp whistle, and gently placed the goblets down.

Asa smiled at the guard's astonishment. He was right. Spending outrageous amounts of money on these old things was ridiculous when that money could be spent on helping others, but Asa was like her mother in this respect. The past needed to be preserved, lest we forget it.

The guard passed out of Asa's view. She opened the armoire door slightly wider so she could hear the guard. To Asa's surprise, she heard yawning, squeaking and rustling, and the sounds of shoes dropping to the floor.

The night watchman was taking a nap!

Now what?

Asa tried remembering the layout of the room. She closed her eyes, trying to visualize it. There were three couches by the back door. That's probably where the guard was.

Closing the door of the armoire, Asa turned on her headlight and put the lock back into place. Inspecting her work, Asa was satisfied no one would be able to tell the lock had been removed.

She just needed to replace that last screw. Taking a deep breath, Asa turned off her light and slid out of the armoire on her belly while holding the quill drawer. Slowly, she wiggled over to the Windsor chair, stopping every now and then, listening for the guard.

He was snoring.

That's a good boy, Asa thought as she reached up, retrieving the last screw. She quickly twisted it in place. Putting on her gloves, she wiped down the drawer before replacing it back in the chair and grabbing the white cloth. Asa crawled over to the stage curtain, slipped under, and let herself out the front door.

She made her way back to the SUV in record time.

Boris looked at his watch. "You're late, Boss. I was getting worried. You run into some trouble?"

"Nothing I couldn't handle," Asa said, peeling off her balaclava mask.

"You got what you needed?"

"Hope so, but if my hunch is correct, it's a motive for murder!"

17

"There are lies, damned lies ... and statistics." That's a quote from Mark Twain, but it certainly resonated with me.

The fact someone went out of their way to lie about me to the police had me in a dither, but that took second place to having Detective Drake accuse me of lying about Rosie. I may be nosy and I may be sneaky, but I'm not a liar.

You—stop laughing.

I do lie, but not for the important stuff.

He hauled me to the police station several times, and each time, I clammed up and waited for Shaneika to come to my rescue.

Was it my fault they couldn't find Rosie? I hadn't seen her since she got out of Dodge, so to speak. I didn't think it was a neighborly thing to do, not that Gage didn't deserve it. He did, but I certainly didn't deserve all the hassle coming my way.

The cosmic question was—if I did know where

Rosie was hiding, would I tell the police? I'm not sure.

Gage had harassed Rosie for years. How much grief can a human being take before they finally lash out at their tormentor? How much should someone be expected to take? I know I would have killed my own stalker if I thought I could have gotten away with it. Fortunately, someone killed him for me, but I can't deny I wanted him dead. Real dead.

So, what are the lies and then the damned lies Twain was talking about? They are the little lies we tell ourselves so we can sleep at night.

I'm a good person. Very few humans are good. Most of us just haven't gotten caught being bad, that's all.

I'm sorry. The only thing most people are sorry about is that they did get caught . . . being bad.

I could never murder. Anyone is capable of murder. Hate and fear are powerful motivators for wanting someone out of the way. Did I mention money and lust as motivators, too?

The good news is that most of us don't kill, but we do ruminate on it from time to time.

Come on now, don't we?

The question is, did Rosie do it?

I don't know, but she wasn't helping her case by disappearing. Wherever Rosie was, the police would catch up with her sooner or later.

And as it turned out, they did.

18

I was in the barn giving Morning Glory a rubdown when I heard the sirens. The piercing sound of the sirens caused Morning Glory to nicker and bob her head in an agitated manner.

"I know, girl. They bother me, too."

When finished, I led her out in the paddock, turning her loose. It was then I saw red and blue lights flashing from June's property. Fearing someone had been hurt, I jumped into my beat-up golf cart and rushed over, but was stopped by a cop at the gate between our two properties.

"I'm sorry, but you can't come in," said the officer.

"What's happened? Is anyone hurt?" I asked, expecting to learn that my daughter had accidentally shot herself in the foot while cleaning her Glock, or June had succumbed to a stroke due to her smoking.

What I did not expect to see was Rosie being led out of the foaling barn in handcuffs by Norbet Drake, nor did I expect to see Charles, also in cuffs, standing by a squad car.

I yelled, "Charles! Charles!"

Hearing his name, Charles looked up in my direction and yelled back, "Josiah, feed Rosie's animals. I'm counting on you."

I didn't get a chance to answer before Charles was placed in the back of a police vehicle and whisked off.

My heart sank.

I knew what this meant.

Charles had hidden Rosie in the foaling barn, which meant he had been arrested for harboring a fugitive.

I zeroed in on the Big House, where I spied Asa, Boris, Bess, and June standing on the pool patio watching.

Did they also know Rosie had been hiding in the barn?

I saw Norbet Drake march up the pathway to the patio, speak with June, and motion to his men.

The gathering retreated inside June's house. Drake followed, after ordering his men to surround the house with one posted at every exit.

I couldn't pass the police barricade, so I had no choice but to return home. It was about six before Bess called to tell me the last police car had exited June's property. I immediately sped over in my little golf cart and joined them by the pool to drown our sorrows in Mint Juleps.

I can honestly say my drink tasted flat.

What had Mark Twain said about lies and damned lies? They sure kill the taste buds.

19

I couldn't stand the silence any longer. "Is anyone going to tell me what's going on?"

Asa took a sip of her watery drink with its melted ice cubes. "I think we are in shock."

"You? In shock, Asa? Was hiding Rosie in the barn your idea?"

"I didn't know, Mother."

I gave her the "I think you are lying big time" mother look.

Turning my attention to June, I said heatedly, "If Charles wasn't alone in hiding Rosie, Drake is going to come back and arrest all of you as accessories, and Lord knows what else he might throw into the soup."

Ignoring me, June leaned over and tapped Boris on the shoulder. "Young man, may I borrow one of your coffin nails?"

Exasperated, I threw my hands up in the air.

June sniffed the cigarette handed to her. "Smells like Turkish tobacco." She looked to Boris for confirmation.

He gave a short nod.

"Bess, are you going to let June smoke cigarettes?"

"Jo, I've got a lot on my mind right now. If Miss June wants to smoke cancer sticks, that's her business. Right now, I'm figuring out how to tell my mother that her husband is not coming home tonight because he's in jail for harboring a fugitive."

June inhaled deeply and blew smoke rings.

"You didn't know?" I asked June.

June's reply was a smoke ring blown into my face.

I coughed a couple times, waving the smoke away.

"I didn't," replied Bess. "Daddy's always had a fondness for Rosie and wanted something done about Gage. I can see him thinking arresting Rosie was a miscarriage of justice."

Asa tapped the patio table. "I think we are missing an important point here."

We gave Asa our undivided attention.

"The question is not that Rosie was hiding in June's barn, but who snitched on her? Whoever snitched on Rosie threw Charles into the mix as well. So again, who fingered Rosie and Charles?"

"Perhaps Charles was with Rosie when the police entered the barn?" I suggested.

"Daddy was in the stallion barn when the police came. I got hold of him via the landline in the barn. Daddy doesn't like to take his phone around the horses. He's afraid he'll accidentally drop it, and a horse will ingest it."

"There's always the chance Mr. Charles didn't know Miss Rosie was here," Boris offered.

It was apparent June didn't want to discuss Charles any longer. She crushed out her half-smoked ciggy. "Bess, don't worry. My lawyer is already working on their behalf. Charles will be home by tomorrow afternoon. You go to your mother. I'll call later."

"Are you sure, Miss June?"

"Absolutely. Now scat. Be with your mother. She must be worried sick."

"Don't worry, Bess. Boris and I will take care of Miss June until this thing is settled. We'll call you if there is a need."

Bess rose. "Miss June's medication is already laid out, and there's plenty of food in the fridge. Labeled quiches and casseroles are in the freezer. All you have to do is thaw them and then bake for thirty minutes at 350 degrees."

"Get going, Bess," June ordered.

"I think I will, but I'll call tomorrow to see how everyone is."

June said, "Vamoose. Get out of here."

"I'll just get my purse and go." Bess gave June one last glance before heading for the Big House.

"I don't know what worries Bess more—her father being arrested or that someone besides herself will be rummaging through her kitchen," June said.

I took a sip of my drink and turned my gaze toward the horse barns in the distance. Had someone working on the farm turned in Rosie with the ultimate goal of getting at Charles? Even that could have a disturbing purpose.

What if their real goal was to gain access to June?

Getting Charles out of the way would certainly make June more vulnerable to jewelry theft, horse tampering, or even kidnapping for ransom.

Boris was apparently thinking along the same lines. He pulled his Glock out and checked the clip.

Asa said, "Miss June, I think we should move you out of the Big House. You shouldn't stay here tonight."

"Folderol!" June waved her hand in the air as if swatting a fly.

"I'm packing a bag for you, and then we're leaving. Don't argue with me," Asa insisted. She hurried into the house while Boris stationed himself where he could observe all entry points to the pool area.

Well! Things certainly got more interesting real fast.

20

Amelia, Bess, and I were sitting in the courtroom for Charles' arraignment. Charles was brought in and sat with the other prisoners waiting for their turn with the judge.

I scanned the room and found Norbet Drake seated behind the Commonwealth DA. I caught his eye and nodded, but he stared back with his lizard eyes, never blinking until the prosecutor whispered to him, causing Drake to turn around.

"All rise."

The three of us jumped to our feet as the judge strode in.

"The Honorable Judge Maureen Lassetter presiding. Be seated."

We sat down and waited until Charles was called. June's lawyer tangled with the DA about the bail amount, but the DA won out. Bail was set at fifty thousand dollars, which meant Charles had to pay ten percent to get out of the hoosegow. He turned and waved to us before being led out of the courtroom.

June's lawyer came and instructed Amelia and Bess to wait downstairs momentarily, as he was going to pay the bail. No doubt, June had instructed him to pay any amount, and Charles would be home before lunch.

Saying a crisp goodbye, Amelia and Bess left, but I stayed for Rosie's arraignment. She wasn't so lucky. She was remanded into custody until her trial and was led from the courtroom sobbing.

Apparently, Gage's influence reached Fayette County. He must have some long arms. Nursing a churning stomach, I picked up my purse and rushed out.

I had to get out of there.

21

I found Kelly where I always find him.

Al's Bar.

I threw my purse into the empty booth seat and sat down beside him, making him scoot over. He shielded his plate from me, but not before I snagged some French fries and dragged them through a mound of ketchup.

"I never have a moment to myself," Kelly mumbled, his eyes shut.

"Hey, whatcha reading?" I asked, picking up a book from his lap. "Short stories by Raymond Carver. Branching out, I see."

"He was also a poet."

"Are you still scribbling out blank verse?"

Kelly looked embarrassed. "Yeah."

"Published yet?"

"Got one poem in the *Kenyon Review*. Comes out next issue."

"*Kenyon Review*. Impressive." I snatched another fry.

"What do you want, Jo?"

"Why is your buddy Norbet Drake riding my bumper?"

"He's a good cop."

"Didn't say he wasn't."

Kelly slapped my hand as I reached for more fries. "If I tell you, will you leave?"

I stuck out my bottom lip the way Asa used to do when I made her eat Brussels sprouts. "You hurt my feelings, Kelly. Makes me want to stick to you like glue until you tell me what I want."

"He's being thorough. Doing his job. He really thinks Rosamond Rose killed Gage Cagle."

"If this case goes to trial, Rosie may have a good chance of getting off because of the self-defense angle."

"I cautioned Drake and the DA to keep in mind that Gage threatened Ms. Rosamond's dogs and made veiled references to killing her on the night of his death."

"But Drake wouldn't listen?"

"He's a kind of black-and-white guy."

"He's not out to get Charles or Lady Elsmere because of personal feelings?"

"I've never known Drake to do anything but strictly by the book. He's got a blemish-free record."

"Tell me something. How would you know about those death threats made by Gage if you're not working on the case?"

"I'm handling all the paperwork for Drake at the station, so I read all the witness statements. When the DA came in to talk with Drake, I happened to be there and gave my two cents worth. There's no conspiracy involved, Josiah. Put your mind at rest."

"Do you know who put the whammy on Charles and Rosie?"

"No, but even if I did, I couldn't tell you."

"If you're handling all the paperwork on the case, how is it you don't know?"

"Drake knows my connection to your family and wouldn't put the name in the case file at the police station. The informant's name is with the DA."

"If Drake feels that way, why hasn't he taken you off the case?"

"Two reasons. We are short-staffed at the moment, and I know most of the players involved. I can winnow through the witness statements quickly."

"Okay. I'll leave you alone. Read your stories." I got up to leave, but Kelly put his hand on my wrist.

"Wait a minute. Is Asa still in town?"

"Why do you ask?"

"No reason. She got something going on with that Slavic gorilla who works for her?"

"Tell your wife hello for me," I said before grabbing my purse and leaving.

22

Passing my barn, I spied Franklin's smart car. I parked my car and hurried inside where I found Hunter saddling his Hanoverian.

We kissed in greeting. Was I ever happy to see him!

"Whatcha up to?" I asked.

"I couldn't stand working on my house any longer and wanted to steal a few hours away. Thought you might want to go horseback riding with me, but you weren't home. I should have called first."

"I was at the courthouse, but I'll tell you about it during our ride. It's been crazy around here."

"Franklin's up at the Big House having tea with Her Ladyship. Looks like the Queen is visiting. There's a security team surrounding the house."

"They're Asa's people. That's what I want to tell you. It's been a wild twenty-four hours."

"Asa, who's supposed to be an insurance fraud agent, has her own security team?"

"Frightening, isn't she?"

"As little contact as I have had with your daughter, I know I would never want to cross her."

"I know her cover story is thin."

"Let's not focus on Batgirl. I want to hear *your* story. Go home and change. I'll bring the horses up to the Butterfly."

"Sounds like a plan." I reached up and kissed Hunter on the lips.

Hunter said, "If you keep kissing me like that, the only thing that's going to happen in this barn is horseplay, and not between the horses."

Laughing, I gave Hunter a playful slap on the shoulder before turning to leave.

"Hey, one more thing before you go."

"Yeah, what's that?"

"Tell me where you've stashed Morning Glory so I can saddle her for you."

"She's in the paddock, Hunter."

"No, she's not."

"I put Glory in the paddock myself yesterday."

"She's not there, Josiah."

I rushed to the paddock, and it was true. Morning Glory was not there. Frantically, I checked all the stalls in the barn, but none of the horses were mine.

"Don't fret, Josiah. One of your hands must have put Morning Glory in a pasture."

"You're probably right."

"I'm going to unsaddle my horse. We can use your

golf cart and check all the fields. Just give me a minute."

Hunter quickly unsaddled his Hanoverian and put the horse in a stall after scooping oats into the horse's bucket. His horse seemed content to stay home and eat.

Following me in his car, Hunter parked in front of the Butterfly, and we jumped into my golf cart and took off.

We checked every one of my pastures. There were horses in them, but no Morning Glory. Hastily we rode over to June's property and checked every pasture, barn, and stall. Nothing.

"What's left?"

"Only the road that leads to the river," I replied, sick with worry.

"Let's try it. She could have wandered to the river for a drink."

We hurried down the bumpy gravel road to the river, but no Morning Glory. Both Hunter and I searched for hoofprints, but saw no sign of them.

We widened our search until it had grown dark and reluctantly headed back to the Butterfly. Since I had cameras around the farm, Hunter wanted to check the video log.

He studied the tapes while I changed and made a quick salad for dinner. The Kitten Kaboodle meowed at the back patio door, so I let them in and fed them before setting the dining table.

"Jo, come look at this," Hunter called.

I hurried to the little cloakroom where I kept all the surveillance equipment.

"Did someone take her?"

"Watch."

Hunter rolled back the tape and played it.

To my amazement, Morning Glory ran around the paddock, gaining speed until she jumped the fence.

"Pintos don't do that! Can't be."

"At least you can relax 'cause it looks like no one stole her."

"She's out there somewhere."

"Having the time of her life." Hunter did his best to reassure me.

"You don't know that. Maybe something spooked her. We've got to find her."

"Let's eat, and then we'll go back out. I'll call the Big House and see if they can spare some men to help us search."

"Good idea."

We ate, but the salad sat like a lump in my throat. I was worried about my horse and was glad when we got back on the road to search for her. Tyrone and Malcolm helped us, but we came back to the house hours later defeated.

No Morning Glory.

With nothing left to do, Hunter went home, pledging to return the next day, but I told him to stay put. I knew searching for Morning Glory would take up valuable time he didn't have at the moment.

Once Hunter left, I was alone at the Butterfly. I had no man. No horse.

Baby and his pet kitty-cats did their best to distract me with scratching the furniture, playing tag, knocking over knickknacks, and regurgitating furballs on my slate floors, but their antics didn't alleviate my worry.

I was in a blue funk and was going to stay that way until I could find my horse—dead or alive.

23

Early the next morning, Marjorie Hughes, a neighbor of Rosie's, called. "Josiah, this is Marge, over by Rosie's place. Do you remember me?"

"Of course, I do. What can I do you for?"

"There's a rumor going 'round that you're missing a horse."

I grabbed the phone tighter. "Yes, ma'am. She jumped the fence yesterday."

"Is she black and white?"

"Yes. Yes. A little pinto."

"I found your horse meandering on the road this morning. She came right up to me. I put her in Gage's cattle field where there's a pond. She looked thirsty. Since Gage's dead and Rosie's in jail, I thought no one would bother her there."

"Marge. Thank you so much. I'll be right over to get her."

"I'm glad. I knew she belonged to someone. Her coat looked really good. You say she jumped over the fence?"

"Can you beat that?"

"Never heard of such a thing. I gotta go to work, but you know where she is . . . that is, if she hasn't jumped the fence again and taken off. Haha."

"Yeah, real funny."

Marge hung up, and I called Hunter with the good news. I could tell he was relieved. He had workmen there, so I got off the phone quick and hurried to Gage's farm, wondering if I would find my black and white pinto when I got there.

Since I didn't own a horse trailer, I threw a rope, bridle, and reins into my golf cart, and off I went. I realized I should have gone next door to borrow a horse trailer with a ramp, but then I'd have to borrow June's dually to pull the horse trailer, and then I'd have to borrow a farmhand who knew how to get a horse in the trailer and drive the truck with the trailer back to my place.

Too much trouble. My thought was that I would tie Morning Glory to the back of my cart and slowly mosey back home. Maybe take a little longer, but no fuss, no muss.

Simple, huh?

I forgot Baby was out doing his business, and when he heard the golf cart whiz by, of course, he jumped into the cart, not wanting to be left behind. "Promise to be good," I begged.

Did I really expect Baby to answer me, much less obey me?

Going to Gage's farm held no anxiety for me. He was dead and gone. I say good riddance.

Charles had taken Rosie's animals back to the Big House, and a neighbor was feeding Gage's cattle. I expected to collect my horse and be back lickity-split.

WRONG!

Baby and I made it to Gage's farm without incident, parking the cart next to the pasture gate. I told Baby to stay in the cart as I got out. "Morning Glory. Glory. Glory. Treat. Treat," I shouted. This usually brought her running.

No whinny. No horse. Just lots of Angus cows chomping on grass.

Suddenly, the flash of a black and white body emerged from the woods that encircled the pasture. I waved wildly so Morning Glory would see me. "Here, girl. Over here. Treat. Got peppermints for ya."

Morning Glory trotted through the cattle herd who lifted their heads to stare as she passed. I held out my hand as Morning Glory came to the gate and stretched her head over to nudge my shoulder. I stroked her muzzle while feeding her peppermints. "You naughty girl. Were you bored? Is that why you jumped the fence? Looking for some adventure, huh?"

Morning Glory nuzzled me, wanting to be scratched behind the ears. I complied for a while until she was relaxed, and I slowly opened the gate wide enough for me to slip through and clipped the lead onto her halter.

She calmly followed me as I led her out and tied the lead to the cart.

Excited, Baby slapped his tail against the seat, but stayed put.

"Now, Glory, we're going home. I'm going to go real slow, but you need to follow when the cart moves. Okay?"

I got into the cart and started down the road at a very slow pace.

Morning Glory resisted by pulling on the lead and bucking. It didn't help when Baby barked at her. "Shut up, Baby. You're making things worse."

It was evident Glory was not willing to walk behind a beat-up golf cart occupied by a harried redhead and a yelping Mastiff.

I sat in the cart not knowing what to do. I thought about walking the horse home, but I knew my leg would give out before I could make it to the barn. I could call Charles and have him send a trailer over. Jumping Jehoshaphat! I left my phone at home.

I would have to put Morning Glory back in the pasture, go home, and get help.

Untying the rope, I led her back inside the gate and unclipped the lead from her rope halter. "I'll be back, Morning Glory. You'll be sleeping in your own stall tonight. I promise."

Hopping into the golf cart, I stepped on the pedal, but the cart didn't move. I turned the key again and pushed the pedal. Nothing. My little cart had finally given up the ghost. Poor shot-up thing.

Now what!

I couldn't walk home. I didn't have my phone, and there were no houses close by. I was at the bottom of a dead-end road. What were my choices?

I looked at Morning Glory who was watching me expectantly, her head hanging over the gate. I had no saddle or mounting block, but I had a bitless bridle, reins, and the cart.

I went over to Morning Glory and petted her neck. "I'm going to have to ride you, Glory. We will go very slow, but I can't walk home like you can, so would you be good enough to carry me?"

Leading Morning Glory out again, I slipped on the bridle, clipped the reins onto her bridle rings, and brought her close to the golf cart. Pushing Baby out of the way, I climbed into the back of the cart and pulled the horse as close as I could. "Please don't shift and cause me to fall."

After giving the pinto several more peppermints, I grabbed the reins and her mane, pulling myself up on her back. Struggling, I got my fanny on her back only to endure the slow process of getting my right leg over her neck to the other side. Not the correct way to get on a horse, but it would have to do. Immediately, I could tell the way I was attempting to get my leg over wasn't going to work.

Being old and infirmed is really a drag.

I would have to try the correct way, which was more stressful for me because of my bad leg. Oh, how I love western saddles with their horns. It's easy to pull oneself up on a horse with a saddle horn. I didn't have anything to hold on to but two strips of leather and a hank of hair.

I needed to get myself higher in order to lower myself on Morning Glory.

Bingo!

There were concrete blocks stacked by the gate. I dragged them over to the cart and made little steps in the back of the cart. It took me about twenty minutes, but the result was worth it. Before I climbed them, I gave Morning Glory the last handful of mints I possessed. "Be good, now, my little pony. Be sweet. I'm counting on you."

Yes, I was bribing an animal. I was that desperate.

Since the pinto was more of a pony size, it wasn't as difficult as I thought it would be. I climbed the steps, which wobbled a bit, but they stayed intact long enough for me to lower myself onto Morning Glory without much stress to herself or me. "Whoa, girl. Easy now. Easy."

I did it!

Sitting on her back for a few minutes, I let Morning Glory adjust to my weight before I gave her the cues to move down the road.

"Baby, come!"

Baby jumped out of the cart and followed behind, sniffing this lump of grass or that mound of manure. Things were going well as we plodded along Rosie's gravel road until we came to an offshoot dirt road.

Morning Glory immediately took a sharp right.

"No girl. That's not the way home." I tugged on the left rein to make the horse turn, but Morning Glory tossed her head in defiance and picked up speed, bouncing me on her back like one of those little rubber balls tied to a wooden paddle. Without stirrups, there was no way I could control my seat, so I was at her mercy, sliding back and forth on her back.

"STOP! WHOA!" I cried, pulling hard on both reins, trying to get Morning Glory to halt. The problem was I didn't have the strength to control this horse, and she knew it. She not only didn't stop, but picked up her pace until we were galloping at full tilt.

Looking ahead, I saw where Morning Glory's path was taking us, grabbed as much of her mane as I could, leaned forward, pressed my legs against her side, and screamed, "Oh, my God, oh, my God!" as we sailed over a fence.

24

I landed with a thump. The wind knocked out of me, I lay in a heap upon the ground, not moving or making a sound.

Was I still alive? Yes, I thought I was.

Was anything broken? Too afraid to move.

Was I bleeding? Hoped not.

I remained in a crumpled lump for what seemed an eternity until my head cleared a little.

Baby whined and circled before stretching out beside me, panting. Occasionally, he pawed me with those sandpaper pads of his, trying to get a response.

I realized he was trying to help, but I heard myself say, "Quit pawing my face, Baby!"

I could speak! At least my mouth worked—the least important part of my body according to some.

Did I have the guts to move? I rolled over on my side. So far, so good.

The first thing I saw was Morning Glory contently munching on grass nearby. The thought came to me that Morning Glory had a future date with a glue factory.

I'd deal with her later. I slowly placed a hand over one eye and then the other. Both worked—no spots or flashes. *Okay*, I thought, *let's sit up.*

Baby was standing now with a waterfall of drool dripping on me. I grabbed his collar and pulled myself up into a sitting position. "Good boy. Good boy." Next, I tried moving my legs. My gams moved. Ribs. Seemed intact.

I wiggled over to a small tree and used it to help me stand. Unbelievable! Could I have really fallen off a horse and not seriously hurt myself?

I slowly took in my surroundings.

Glory had thrown me on a part of Gage's farm I had never visited before. Through the trees, I could see the top of a building and electrical wires going to it. That meant the building had electricity and perhaps a phone.

"Baby, come."

Hobbling down a faint pathway, I came to a clearing where some sort of workshop stood with a pickup in front. "Hello! Hello! I need help. Anyone there? Hello?"

Hurrying as fast as I could, which wasn't swift by any means, and with Baby faithfully by my side, I finally reached the truck and, opening its door, honked the horn. "Hello. Can you help me please? I fell off my horse."

No one appeared at the door of the workshop.

I stood listening. No sounds of machinery came from the shop—just birds chirping, squirrels rustling in the trees, and cows lowing in the distance, not to mention the sounds from a cloud of flies buzzing around my head. I swatted at them, mystified at their number. Up in the hazy sky, several buzzards lazily swirled on the wind currents. Flies and buzzards—portents of death, but I didn't catch on.

I could hear a radio faintly playing inside as I knocked loudly on the door. Someone had to be near. I waited, but no one came. Determined to see if a phone was handy, I twisted the doorknob and pushed the door. The weather-beaten door fought me, but using my hip, I pushed it open. That's when the smell hit me. Actually, stench would be a better choice of words.

Baby's brow furrowed, and he emitted a high-pitched whine.

I'm not ashamed to say I vomited. I think it was due more to the revulsion I felt rather than the physical effect the strong odor had on me.

After emptying my guts, I sat in the truck with Baby, wondering what to do. I refused to mount Morning Glory again, but I had to get help.

With no way around it, I was going to have to enter the workshop and look for car keys or a phone. Finding a somewhat clean bandana in the front seat of the truck, I wrapped it around my face, covering my nose and mouth.

"Stay here," I ordered Baby, and taking a deep breath, I ventured inside the workshop. I tried to ignore the smell, but I was gagging.

The shop was dark and dank. I felt for a light switch just inside the door and turned on the lights. That's when I spied a cell phone on a workbench. Thank the Lord!

Grabbing it, I rushed outside. The phone had some juice left; not much, but enough to make one call. I punched in three numbers.

"Hello? 911? I need to report a death. There's been a murder!"

25

Asa helped me into the clothes she brought to the hospital from the Butterfly. The clothes I was wearing had been bagged and tagged by the Sheriff's Department.

The emergency doctor came in the cubicle and pulled the curtain shut. "Good news. No internal injuries."

"What about the CAT scan?" Asa asked.

"Clean. Aside from bruising and minor cuts, you're okay, Mrs. Reynolds. You'll be stiff for a couple of days, to be sure, but other than that you'll be fine. You can leave."

I asked, "So, I'm free to go?"

"Fine with me."

"But not with me."

Asa, the ER doctor, and I turned our eyes toward the door as the Sheriff and one of his minions entered the room with Detective Drake close behind them, bringing up the rear.

"This murder happened in Jessamine County, not Fayette. Detective Drake, aren't you out of your jurisdiction?" Asa inquired, helping me climb off the examination table.

"The Sheriff called me to share the information that you stumbled upon yet another body, and within a month's time, I might add, Mrs. Reynolds."

"Ain't I a lucky girl?" I snarled.

"Mrs. Reynolds, good luck. I'll leave you to it," the doctor said, giving the three lawmen a wide berth when exiting.

"Thanks, Doc," I said, slipping into a wheelchair the nurse had brought. "Excuse me, gentlemen, but any statement from me will have to wait. I'm going home to a hot bath and a soft bed."

The Sheriff blocked my way. "We're not here for a statement. We're here for evidence."

"What evidence? The only thing I can tell you is that I fell off my horse and needed a phone. I found the workshop, bada bing. Discovered a dead body with something sticking out of its neck. Called the police. Thus, here I am. That's my statement. Now I want to go home."

"We have a court order to collect your clothes, fingerprints, debris under your fingernails, and DNA."

"You already have my clothes. Two sets of clothes, I might add. I guess I'm never going to get my Dior dress back."

"And we are going to get your fingerprints and DNA as well."

"Let me see the warrant," Asa demanded.

The Sheriff handed Asa an official-looking document, which she scanned.

"Mom, you're going to have to do as they ask. It's a court order."

"You think a middle-aged beekeeper with a bum leg killed two men within a month? If you considered me a suspect, Drake, you wouldn't have arrested Rosamond Rose."

"This second murder gives me pause. Might have to rethink the case," Drake said.

"I guess we're even then because you give me indigestion." There was no point fighting them. I was going to have to obey the court order or face a charge of contempt. "Just my luck to find two stiffs, huh? Can we do this here?"

The Sheriff threw a case on the examination table. "Yep. Shouldn't take more than a few minutes, little lady."

"Then can I go home?"

"Yep, it's all we require for now."

"Dreamy."

"Open wide," the Sheriff said as he swabbed my mouth.

Drake looked on with smug satisfaction.

I was beginning to truly loathe that guy.

26

"Where's Glory?" I asked, fluffing my pillows. I was now back at the Butterfly and enjoying sleeping in my own bed.

Asa replied, "She's still at Gage's place."

"I need to get her out of there and bring her home."

"Charles will take care of it. Don't worry."

"You haven't called Hunter, have you?" I asked Asa.

"No. Should I?"

"I'd rather you didn't. He's on the verge of selling Wickliffe Manor and shouldn't have any interruptions."

"You think Hunter's time fixing his wreck of a house is more important than learning you were thrown off a horse he bought for you? Shouldn't he be informed this untamed beast likes to jump fences and is dangerous?"

"I'll tell him, but not right now."

"It's your funeral. Here, eat this soup. I made it myself."

"Oh, lovely," I replied, trying not to show my dismay.

Asa was a *good* many things, but a *good* cook was not one of them.

"I'm going to turn on one of those old movies you love. You relax. I'll take care of everything."

Asa turned on *Cape Fear* with Robert Mitchum and Gregory Peck. Robert Mitchum played Max Cady, a serial rapist stalking Gregory Peck's family. Not exactly a family movie, but I found it relaxing as I knew Max Cady was going to get his comeuppance. Not every bad guy in the real world gets his due, but they do in the movies.

As soon as Asa left my bedroom, I gave the soup to Baby, who was lying next to me with his pets, the Kitty Kaboodle, crawling all over him.

Asa was right. Seeing an old black and white movie from 1962 was calming, and I was soon sleeping the sleep of the angels.

27

The Sheriff, whose name was Wilbur Smedley, met Shaneika at the front door.

"Thank you for coming, Sheriff," Shaneika said.

"No problem. I've always wanted to see the Butterfly," the Sheriff replied, taking off his Stetson.

"Mrs. Reynolds is in here." Shaneika led the Sheriff into the great room where I sat at my Nakashima table.

"Hello, Sheriff," I said. "Thank you for not making me come to the Sheriff's Department."

"Like I told this lady here, glad to."

"How may I help you?"

Wilbur Smedley opened his briefcase and laid five photographs before me. "Can you identify any of these men, Mrs. Reynolds?"

I picked up each photograph and carefully studied it. Pointing to one, I said, "I've seen this man before. He was the deputy who came with you to the hospital."

Wilbur smiled but didn't respond.

I tapped on another picture. "This peculiar little

man was at the auction. He was wearing a rumpled suit and seemed very agitated during the auction. Afterward, I saw him arguing with Gage Cagle and Eli Owsley."

"Any idea what they were fighting about?"

"I was too far away to hear, but a young lady by the name of Deliah Webster was taking pictures at the event. She snapped a photo of them quarreling."

"How do I get in touch with this Deliah Webster?"

Shaneika spoke up. "I can get the photo for you, Sheriff."

If Wilbur Smedley was surprised, he didn't show it. "By tomorrow?"

"If you like," Shaneika responded.

"You've never seen this man before the auction, Mrs. Reynolds?"

"No."

"Did you get a good look at the corpse in the workshop?"

"Not really. Just a quick glance. The smell was so awful."

"You said in your statement that you went into the shop a second time. Can you tell me why?"

"I have a bad leg and had fallen off my horse. I was pretty shaken up. I needed help and thought I could find a phone or the keys to the truck parked outside. Luckily, I found a cell phone on the worktable. I guess it was the dead man's."

"It sure was. Weren't you scared the killer might still be around?"

"It didn't cross my mind because it was obvious the body had been there for some time."

"Yep, he was pretty ripe with the heat and all."

"Besides, I had my dog with me."

"Is that the same dog that charged my men?" Smedley asked, thumbing at Baby lying in the sunlight on the slate floor, snoring.

"That must have been one of Rosie's dogs," I lied.

"Uh-huh."

Shaneika asked, "Sheriff, is the man whom Mrs. Reynolds identified in your photo the same man found dead in the workshop?"

Wilbur Smedley stood and gathered the photographs, storing them in his briefcase. He put on his Stetson cowboy hat and tipped its brim in salutation. "Y'all been a big help. I'm much obliged. Ladies, good day to ya both," he said and was out the door before two shakes of a lamb's tail.

I turned to Shaneika. "Something stinks in Denmark."

"And it ain't the cheese," she replied.

Whatever it was, I wasn't going to sit on my laurels and wait for the police to come after me.

I was going to do something about it, and if need be, lie through my teeth.

28

I waited until mid-morning when most people were at work before I gallivanted over to Gage's workshop. Charles had loaned me one of his electric carts, which was great, as no one would hear the golf cart and look out their windows. I was trying to be sneaky.

Arriving at the workshop, I scanned the tree line, looking for cameras the police might have secreted. Seeing none, I climbed under the crime scene tape and stopped at the front door.

The tape stretched across the door had been sliced at the doorjamb.

That's not good!

Someone had been here before me and might still be in the workshop, but there was no sign of a vehicle, and it had rained the night before. I hadn't seen any fresh tracks in the moist soil.

Should I take a chance, believing some nosey neighbor had come by to check out the crime scene before the rain, or should I err on the side of caution, assuming a bad guy could be lurking inside?

I was alone in a desolate area except for a few dozen cows. I decided to be a coward. It was time to abort the mission.

I was turning to leave when the door violently tore open, causing me to jump and bolt twenty feet before I heard, "Hello, Mother!"

"Jumping Jehoshaphat! You gave me a start," I huffed.

Asa stood in the doorway with an amused expression on her face. "Didn't mean to."

"Sure, you did, Asa. You need to control that nasty streak in you. You've only got one mother."

"You want to come in or not? You can berate my dark side another time."

"Why are you here?"

"Why are you here?"

"Snooping," I answered.

"Same here." Asa pushed the door open all the way and beckoned. "Well, come on in, partner in crime."

"Thank you veeerrry veeerrry much," I replied in a British accent.

"Don't mention it," Asa said in a French accent.

"What are you looking for?"

"What are you looking for?"

"Answering my question with the same question is becoming very thin, Asa."

"Is that very thin or veeerrry veeerrry thin?"

"I can still put you over my knee, young lady."

"With that threat, I'd better behave then."

"How long have you been here?"

Asa said, "Long enough to piece together a theory."

"Want to let your feeble old mother in on it?"

"There's one piece of evidence still missing."

I asked, "Will it prove Rosie didn't kill Gage?"

"Possibly."

"But not one hundred percent?"

Asa shook her head. "Afraid not."

"The police didn't take much," I said, looking around the shop.

"It's obvious they checked for prints and took DNA samples."

"This place looks like a wood workshop," I mused while wandering about. "That's a huge stack of wood stored here. Looks old." I leaned over to smell and touch the wood.

"It's all reclaimed wood. Probably a couple hundred years old. Since farmers are tearing down their tobacco barns, it's easy wood to obtain."

"I know barn wood is valuable, but what would Gage want with it? He wasn't handy with crafts. His hobby was making Rosie miserable."

"I think that question is the crux of his murder."

"Hmm."

"What else do you see, Mother?"

I walked about the shop, studying the contents.

"The floor is covered with debris and wood shavings, but here and there I see a concrete pad underneath, so this shop is very old and looks like it hasn't been cleaned since Truman was in the White House."

"Go on."

"There are several large workbenches with tools."

"What about the tools?"

I was about to examine one of the tools when Asa handed me a pair of gloves. "Fingerprints, Mother. Fingerprints."

"Thank you, Asa. Umm, let me see. The workbenches all have electrical outlets. I know the outlets work as the lights are on, and when I was here before I heard a radio—that radio." I pointed to a grungy beige 1970s clock radio stuck on a ledge near an outlet. "But I don't see any power tools."

"What else?"

"The tools look ancient. Probably nineteenth or even eighteenth-century woodworking tools. They have been recently used as many of them have sharpened metal edges, and an oil has been applied to the wooden handles."

"Look over here," said Asa, pulling a tarp back.

Underneath the tarp was an antique sugar chest sitting on top of a small Chippendale side table. Beyond them, I could see lots of "fancy" chairs in various states of disrepair.

The musty air under the tarp had a familiar scent. "I smell anise."

Asa held up a grimy bag filled with black licorice sticks.

"I hope you're not going to eat any of those."

"Nope. I'm going to put them back where I found them," Asa said, sliding open the drawer of the sideboard and dropping the bag of candy into it. She carefully replaced the dusty tarpaulin again. "What's your conclusion, Mother?"

I laughed so loud the birds took to the air from the trees in alarm.

Could the answer be this simple? It was so absurd.

"It appears Gage Cagle was hoisted with his own petard."

In other words, Gage *done got himself kilt* because he bid on his own counterfeit antiques.

29

"I caused the death of Gage because I dropped the Windsor chairs on him?" Lady Elsmere asked, flabbergasted.

"Eli Owsley and the other man were arguing with Gage because he wasn't supposed to be at the auction, let alone join in the bidding, but Gage couldn't refuse the opportunity to gloat. He wanted Rosie to know he had been released, and the PO had been thrown out, not to mention bidding up the price on the chairs to stick it to you," Asa said.

June dropped ashes down her dress from the cigarette she had been smoking.

"Give that disgusting thing to me," I groused, snatching her cancer stick and crushing it in the ashtray.

June suggested, "Surely, you don't think Rosie killed the man discovered in the shop?"

Asa handed June a cup of tea. "She was in jail at the time he was murdered."

"And Gage?"

Asa glanced at me. "I don't know, Miss June. She could have."

"If Eli Owsley was in on this forgery, he could have killed Gage and the man arguing with Gage at the auction."

"At the moment, we don't know if the third man at the auction is the same man found dead in the workshop, as the autopsy report hasn't come back yet. In reference to your question, Mr. Owsley could have killed Gage, but no evidence points to him," Asa replied.

"Please, go over it again," June said. "It's so confusing."

"I think Gage was part of a group that forged eighteenth and nineteenth-century Kentucky furniture. The man killed recently was the woodworker who made the furniture on Gage's property. Gage was the middleman, and Eli Owsley fronted the furniture through his Cincinnati retail shop and auctions. It's one of the reasons Gage harassed Rosie. He didn't want her near the workshop. It was the center of operations for all his nefarious dealings. Mother and I even found an old still there, so he was making moonshine at one time," Asa said.

I added, "You said yourself Gage was always flirting with the wrong side of the law."

June asked, "But why forge antiques? Nobody

wants antiques anymore but old relics like myself."

"Not true," I said. "Period Kentucky-made furniture is going through the roof with East Coast collectors because of its rarity."

"Still doesn't make sense. If that is true, why sell those Porter Clay chairs in Lexington? Why not sell them at Christies or Sotheby's in New York?"

"Because of you, Miss June. How many people did you tell you wanted to start a Kentucky museum?"

"A few."

"You were the mark. Eli Owsley keeps a dossier on all his clients. He knew you would salivate at the thought of snaring rare comb-back Windsor chairs made by Porter Clay. It would have been an exceptional find, indeed."

"Me and my big mouth."

Turning to Asa, I asked, "What are you going to do now?"

"Keep digging. This is all conjecture for the moment. Finding Eli Owsley's fingerprints in the workshop would go a long way to providing the proof needed. That would tie the three of them together."

"The Sheriff already dusted for fingerprints," June reminded Asa.

"But I bet only the door, the tools, and the workbenches were fingerprinted. The murderer would have wiped his fingerprints from those areas but forgotten where else he might have put his hands if he visited other times."

"A compelling scenario. Let's go get him," I said.

Asa cocked her head and asked, "How?"

I gave her a greasy smile and proposed, "If June was the mark, let's turn the tables on Eli and use June to beat Eli at his own game."

Asa's eyes sparkled as she turned them upon June, who drew back in alarm. "Yes, let's."

30

"Lady Elsmere, your offer is generous, but the chairs belong to Gage Cagle's estate," professed Eli Owsley, flitting about the storage room of the auction house, yelling instructions at workmen.

"He's dead."

"Yes, but he made the final offer on the chairs."

Asa interrupted, "Did Mr. Cagle pay for the chairs?"

"Of course, he did."

"Are you sure, Mr. Owsley? When did he have time to pay for them? He was murdered shortly after the bidding."

"He gave me a check."

"May I see the check, please?"

"I've already cashed it, so you see the chairs are the property of Mr. Cagle's estate." He turned his back and whisked off the shade of a Tiffany floor lamp, draping it in thick bubble wrap.

"Refund Cagle's estate and sell me the chairs," insisted June.

Asa asked, "Why were you and Willow Cherry arguing with Gage Cagle?"

Eli Owsley froze. "Who?"

"Willow Cherry. You know, the man who was murdered on Gage's property last week. Here's his picture." Asa pulled a newspaper article out of her pocket and showed it to Mr. Owsley.

Flustered, Mr. Owsley peeked at the newspaper article and said, "Sorry, I don't know that man."

"Sure you do," insisted Asa as she pulled Deliah's picture of the three men arguing from her other coat pocket.

Mr. Owsley peered over his glasses at the photo. "I don't know what you think you're doing, but I don't know that man."

"The Jessamine County Sheriff's Department is going to comb Gage's workshop dusting for fingerprints. They have a theory that you, Willow Cherry, and Gage Cagle were working together. If they find even a partial print of yours in Gage's workshop, you're toast. It would prove you three were working together."

"Ladies, please excuse me, but I have work to do."

June reached out a bejeweled hand to clutch Eli's arm. "Are you going to sell me those chairs or not?"

Eli Owsley gave June a look of disbelief before scurrying away.

"He didn't break," June said.

"Let's see if he falls for the fingerprint ruse."

"Perhaps he didn't have anything to do with Willow Cherry's death?"

"Everything points to Eli Owsley as the killer, Miss June. I tell you he did it."

June chuckled. "Willow Cherry. What a name."

Asa agreed. "Who could make this stuff up? Not any mystery writer, that's for sure."

31

Since my daughter had deemed me a distraction, I wasn't allowed to accompany Asa and June on their little adventure. There was nothing for me to do but check on my animals.

My bees seemed fine. I pulled out a ratty chair I kept at the apiary and studied them for an hour or so. There were no signs of the bees robbing each other's hives, and they were bringing in dark yellow and orange pollen on their pollen baskets located on their hind legs. House bees met them at the entrance to transfer the nectar from the field bees to storage in the hive. Once the pollen and nectar were reassigned to the house bee, the field bee was winging her way again to another nectar source.

"No rest for the weary," my mother would always say.

I say, "Don't be busy as a bee, because you'll work yourself to death."

Speaking of those working themselves to death,

Hunter had called earlier, saying he was coming over. I looked at my watch. He should be in the barn by now. Reluctantly, I put away my chair and bid my babies goodbye.

I trudged through the field over to the barn, scattering several goats, sheep, one nasty llama who spat at me, and several broken-down horses no one wanted any longer—society's cast-offs. They had a home with me until they died. For the time being, I had the money to feed them and was glad to do so.

It was interesting to me that the goats and the horses hung out together while the llama and the sheep made a little community of their own. I guess the two species that were periodically shorn had grown an affinity for each other.

When I got to the barn, Hunter was leaning on the fence watching Morning Glory and his Hanoverian in the paddock.

"What's up, doc?"

Hunter greeted me with a kiss and a hug. The day was looking up.

"Nicest thing that's happened to me all day."

"Glad you think so, Miss Josiah, but I've got some news that will make you smile wider."

"I'm listening."

"I called the former owner of Morning Glory and told him what happened. He explained that Morning Glory was trained to respond to the rider shifting in the saddle and knee pressure cues. She was never taught to respond to reins."

"When I've ridden her before she followed rein cues."

"I bet she didn't. You were riding with my horse and me. I think she did whatever the Hanoverian did. Now, before you argue with me, think about it."

"I'm not arguing with you."

"Every time you've ridden Glory, we were together. Right?"

"Yeah."

"I think she was ignoring the rein cues and just following my horse. The other day you were riding bareback without a blanket, so she was sensitive to your movement on her back and the pressure from your knees."

"And I couldn't keep my seat, so I confused her when I was sliding back and forth on her back. She was trying to follow what she thought was my direction. Baffled, she panicked."

Hunter said, "I think that's what happened. It was a miracle both of you weren't hurt."

"I hope I'm first on that list."

"Feeling a little insecure today?"

I batted my eyelashes. "Yes, doctor. Can you help me?"

"I would love to," Hunter murmured.

"Oh, doctor! I believe you're thinking something nasty."

"I sure am," Hunter said, grabbing me around the waist and pulling me into the barn.

I squealed with delight until we encountered Malcolm bringing in my boarded horses for the night.

"Get a room," Malcolm mumbled as he passed by.

Hunter and I burst out laughing as we hurried to his car and buzzed out of there.

32

"Can we go to Wickliffe Manor?"

"Franklin's home and supposed to be painting the shutters. That's why I have his car."

"We can't go back to the Butterfly. Boris *Whatshisface* is there, working on something for Asa."

"What about Matt's house?"

"If Asa sees a car at the house, she'll investigate, and I'm not sure when she'll be back."

"We certainly don't want that."

"No, we don't."

"It's pretty sad when two consenting adults with three residences between them can't be alone."

"Not to mention several barns."

"Pitiful."

"Let's get something to eat," I suggested.

"I have another appetite that needs feeding."

"Perhaps when you sell Wickliffe Manor, we can go away for the weekend? Some place nice."

"The deal fell through. My buyer backed out."

I patted Hunter's shoulder in sympathy. "I'm sorry.

Are you going to file for bankruptcy?"

"I've got several jobs lined up next month. It will keep the wolf from the door for now, but I'll be out of town for several weeks."

"I'll get by. You do what you have to do."

"Thanks for being so understanding."

"That's what girlfriends do."

"They do?"

"Yep."

"You know what else girlfriends do?"

"Keep your eyes on the road, buster. At your age, you'd think the libido would calm down."

"You bring out the *wolf* in me." Hunter opened his window and howled at passing cars.

"I haven't had fun like this for the longest time," I said. "I have one more question about Glory. What is with jumping fences? Pintos don't jump."

"Again, this is something the owner didn't bother to tell me when I bought her. He said she takes a notion now and then and jumps anything in her path. She likes to."

"I can't ride Glory anymore. I don't trust her."

"I have a buddy who works with jumpers. I'll ask him what to do with Glory. Don't ride her until we retrain her."

"I was thinking, Hunter."

"That's unusual."

"Funny. No really. The night Glory jumped the fence, your horse wasn't in the paddock with her.

Malcolm had taken your horse over to June's farm to see the vet as one of his legs had some swelling. He didn't bring her back until the next morning."

"I bet Glory jumped the fence looking for my horse, since they seem to be in this co-dependent relationship."

"Enough of the psycho-babble, Herr Doctor Wickliffe. It's true though. Glory feels anxious when she can't see your horse, and that's what sets her off, I'll bet."

"You're probably right, but she's safe now, and my horse is with her, so can you put your mind at rest?"

I kidded, "I will think only of you tonight, Hunter. You're my reason for living."

"I wish that were true," Hunter grumbled. "Move closer, woman. I'm gonna open the windows and let the wind rush through our hair."

"What there is of it."

"You're spoiling the mood, Josiah."

"Sorry."

"As I was saying, I'm gonna put my arm around you and turn on some sophomoric music and cruise until we find a deserted lane where I'm going to park, and we're going to neck."

"In this tiny car?"

Hunter sighed as he turned the car down a dusty lane.

What did I say earlier about it being prudent to keep one's thoughts to oneself sometimes?

33

Hunter turned down my driveway but pulled up short in front of the Butterfly. Two Jessamine County Sheriff Department vehicles were smack-dab in front of my house.

I stumbled out of the car as Asa rushed over. "Where have you been? I've been worried."

Giggling, I sneaked a peek at Hunter.

Embarrassed, he sheepishly looked away.

Shouldn't I have been the one blushing?

Asa leaned forward and sniffed. "Have you been drinking?"

"Naw."

Asa sniffed again. "You have been drinking! I smell liquor on your breath."

I hate being lectured by my daughter and segued to another topic. "Why have the fuzz gathered at my house?"

"That's why I've been trying to get hold of you, but a certain middle-aged mother turned her phone off."

"Has there been a break in the case?"

"Sheriff Smedley liked my idea of setting up cameras in and around the workshop, and we set the plan in motion this afternoon. Owsley took the bait about dusting for additional fingerprints. He's trying to remove all evidence that might connect him to Willow Cherry and Gage Cagle, and we're getting it on tape."

"But why are they here?" I asked, pointing to the deputies' cars.

"The Sheriff's Department needed a base of operation. I tried calling you, but apparently, you were indisposed." Asa shook my shoulders. "Mother, Eli Owsley took the bait June and I set. He's at Gage's workshop right now."

"I've got to see this. Come on, Hunter."

Hunter said, "I've got to get back, Jo. Talk to you tomorrow?"

I nodded, and Hunter got into the smart car and flew down the road, spraying gravel everywhere.

"I really need to have my driveway paved," I murmured, "but too expensive. Asa, you sure know how to kill a mood." I was speaking to the air for Asa had returned to the house, so I dutifully followed her inside.

In my coat closet where I kept my security monitors, Boris and the Sheriff were sitting and making notes. Apparently, Asa had tied the workshop cameras into my system.

Several deputies hung around the door, peeking

inside. They pulled back when Asa pushed her way into the room. It was tight quarters is all I could say.

I poked my head in. "What's happening?"

Boris answered, "Owsley's been wiping down objects, and now he's taking furniture from under the tarp and loading the pieces in his trailer."

"As soon as he passes through the main gate onto the county road, my boys will pick Mr. Fancy Pants up. They're hiding down the road, just beyond Cagle's property line."

I thought the moniker Mr. Fancy Pants odd, but kept my mouth shut. See? I use common sense once in a while.

Asa mused, "This is peculiar behavior. Mr. Owsley knows your department has taken inventory of everything in the shop, so why come back and remove the furniture? He's begging to be caught."

"Because he thinks we're dumb country hicks, Miss Asa. We're not smart enough to put two and two together, and he's smarter than anyone in law enforcement. Comes down to ego. Simple ego," Sheriff Smedley informed her.

"I've met his cousins," Asa kidded.

Boris seemed confused. "You have captured his cousins?"

"Just an expression, Boris. I've met criminals like Owsley who think they can never be apprehended," Asa explained.

"Ah."

"In other words, Owsley got too big for his britches," Sheriff Smedley said, kidding the big Eastern European galoot.

Boris shook his head, saying, "I don't see what little pants have to do with anything."

I pointed at one of the monitors. "Owsley's taking off!"

Sheriff Smedley spoke into his radio, "Boys, he's coming your way."

Boris pressed a button on a computer attached to the monitors and handed a thingamajig to the Sheriff. "Here's the proof you need."

The Sheriff put it in a sealed envelope and dated it. "You got a backup?"

Boris nodded.

"Good man."

Putting on his Stetson, Sheriff Smedley passed by me and motioned to his men. They ran out the door and jumped into their vehicles. Before leaving, Sheriff Smedley said to me, "Grateful for your help, ma'am. Won't forget."

Asa followed. "Are you going to let me know what happens? After all, it was *my* idea."

Sheriff Smedley waved goodbye before ducking into one of the vehicles. Sirens blasting and lights flashing, the cars rushed down my driveway spraying gravel everywhere.

"I really, really need to get that driveway paved," I murmured before heading back into the house.

34

Asa and Boris were still bivouacked at the Big House.

I hadn't had breakfast yet, so this was the perfect time to drop by unannounced. "Hello, everyone."

Bess had laid out a traditional English breakfast, complete with kippers, in the breakfast room, which looked out over June's vast estate. There's nothing like being able to sit there and eat strawberry scones with clotted cream while watching the colts play with each other in the fields.

"You're up early," June said, picking up her coffee cup.

I threw the newspaper on the table. "Thought you might like to see this."

Asa grabbed the paper off the table and skimmed the front page.

"What does it say?" asked June, reaching for it.

Asa kept the paper out of June's reach. "I'll read it to you."

Eli Owsley, 52, owner of Owsley Antique Emporium, 150 Longleaf Drive, Cincinnati, Ohio, was arrested for the murder of Willow Cherry, 48, Nicholasville, Kentucky. It is alleged that both Owsley and Cherry conspired to reproduce antique Kentucky furniture, selling the pieces to the public as authentic and original.

Mr. Cherry died from blunt force trauma to the head. In addition, he was stabbed with an antique screwdriver that pierced his lung.

Eli Owsley confessed to the death of Willow Cherry, pleading it was self-defense, as Mr. Cherry attacked him.

The Jessamine County District Attorney has no comment as to whether a plea deal has been reached at this time.

The case against Mr. Owsley is being further investigated by the Lexington Police Department, as it is believed a third accomplice, Gage Cagle, 82, Nicholasville, Kentucky was murdered. Gage Cagle died from loss of blood due to a stab wound to his femoral artery in his left leg.

While Mr. Owsley has confessed to the death of Willow Cherry, he denies having been the cause of Gage Cagle's demise.

In light of the arrest of Eli Owsley, District Attorney, Leanne Bluestocking, says further investigation in the murder of Gage Cagle is warranted.

Rosamond Rose, initially arrested for the murder of Gage Cagle, has been released from custody and is no longer considered a person of interest in the case.

Mr. Cagle's murder investigation is still ongoing at the posting of this article.

"Have you talked to Rosie?" I asked June.

"No, but Charles has. Rosie's back at her house with her animals again. Charles took over groceries and casseroles so she doesn't have to go out. She told Charles she wants to be alone until some of the notoriety from the case dies down."

"I can understand her desire for privacy," Asa said, filling a plate with scrambled eggs, biscuits and gravy, and hot cakes from the sideboard. She artfully placed four strips of bacon on the side to create a symmetrical arrangement.

The apple didn't fall from the tree.

"Rosie told Charles she's turning off the phone and doing nothing but sleeping for a couple of days. Charles put a lock on the main gate, giving the key to Rosie. That way no one can come on Gage's property without Rosie's permission."

"What's going to become of Gage's property?" Asa asked as she poured syrup over her hotcakes.

June mentioned quickly, "He has no direct descendants. I might pick it up for a song."

"What would you want with it?" I asked, filling up a plate with eggs and scones.

"The property sits at the back of a quiet road. No

houses around except for Rosie's. Charles has always wanted a place to put abandoned grazing animals as part of his mission on the Humane Society Board. I might give the land to him as a Christmas present."

Asa said, "Then Charles has to pay the taxes, up-keep the land, pay for feed himself. Keep it in your name, and your corporation can pay for everything and consider it a tax deduction."

"Make the sanctuary a DBA of your farm corporation. He'll become the owner eventually," I added.

"What misery are you three planning to put my daddy through now?" asked Bess, checking the coffee and orange juice.

June assured, "It's something Charles will enjoy."

"You're not still considering dragging him into the crazy museum idea of yours?"

"No," June pouted.

Bess gave June a stern once-over before leaving.

Asa folded her napkin. "This has been great fun, folks, but I'm heading back to New York today."

"Well, thanks for letting me know," I replied, irritated.

June sulked, "Sorry to see you leave so soon."

"Soon? I've been here much longer than I anticipated, but it's been fun, girls. Now, Mother, don't look like that. After what I saw the other day, I'd just be in the way."

June snapped her head toward me. "What's she talking about?"

Asa sang, "Josiah and Hunter sitting in a tree. K-I-S-S-I-N-G!"

"Do tell me all the details, Josiah. Is it love or is it lust? Have you done the nasty? If yes, is Hunter any good?"

"See what you started, Asa?" I complained.

"Do you notice, Miss June, that Mother is not denying anything happened?"

"Yes, I do, Asa."

"My lovely dears, it's been great, but I must be off."

"Are you taking the hunky Boris, or are you leaving him for me?" June hinted.

"He's already at the airport with the luggage."

"I certainly hope you gave him leave to eat breakfast," I commented.

Asa made a face and swept out the door.

I know I don't like hugs, but a kiss on the cheek would have been sweet, or an "I love you, Mom."

Resigned, I took a sip of my orange juice. My relationship with Asa was what it was.

35

The light fell a little left of noon, but Hunter was hungry. He had spent most of the morning cutting down honeysuckle bushes, which were threatening to take over the pastures near a patch of woods. While the deep South had kudzu as a biological threat, Kentucky had honeysuckle to deal with. He was hot, sweaty, and tired. Coming in the back way, he opened the screen door and was met by Asa making a turkey sandwich.

"You should keep your doors locked."

"Locked doors have never stopped you before, Asa. To what do I owe the pleasure?"

Asa held her sandwich out to Hunter. "Want me to make you one? I'm so hungry, and I had breakfast just a short while ago. Must be the country air."

"I want to know what you're doing here."

"Got any spicy mustard? Maybe a craft beer?"

Hunter retrieved a bottle of yellow mustard and a soft drink out of the fridge. "Best I can do."

"Thanks," Asa replied, taking a swig of her drink.

"Ah, that's better. I was so thirsty."

"Asa! You didn't come here to have lunch."

Asa tore her sandwich into smaller pieces. "I've come to save your farm."

"How is that?"

"You've got a treasure trove of stuff here that will do well on the open market, especially the auction houses in New York or Boston."

"I've already gone down that road when Franklin was arrested. No one wants silver tea services or old antiques but little old ladies and their ranks are rapidly thinning."

"Ah, ye of little faith. When I was snooping around your place when Madison Smythe died here, I noticed some things."

"Like what?"

"You do understand I am an art insurance investigator?"

"If you say so."

"I do. Getting back to the subject at hand, the dusty old Kentucky longrifle over the fireplace in your office was made by John Bonewitz of Pine Grove, Pennsylvania, probably circa 1778 to 1809. There's one on the market right now being sold by a private collector for sixty-five thousand dollars."

Hunter sat at the table and munched on part of Asa's sandwich. "I'm listening."

"Everything about your rifle is true down to Bonewitz's trademarks on the barrel. If you can find some documentation like a letter written by your illustrious ancestors mentioning the rifle, a daguerreotype of a family member holding the rifle, or a bill of sale, the price will go up even more."

"What do I do?"

"Never clean the gun. Leave it as it is, but I would insure it for a hundred thousand dollars."

"Is there anything else?"

"In the cupboard near the back stairs, I counted over a hundred antique Kentucky Derby glasses. They go for a pretty penny. You can sell those yourself as a lot or individually on the internet."

"I was going to donate those to a charity."

"Big mistake. You don't realize what you have here is a time capsule. There is one particular tea service crammed behind some other silver in the butler's pantry."

"Oh, that one. My mother hated it, so it was never used."

"Your mother's ugly duckling teapot is worth a small fortune as it was made by Ann Bateman, circa 1770-1800. Everyone thinks of Paul Revere as the premier American silversmith, but a tea service made by a member of the Bateman family would command a serious price tag." Asa looked at her watch. "Look, I've gotta go, or I'll miss my plane. I left a list of items and the names of appraisers who work in those particular fields on your desk. They will help you get the best price if you want to sell. Do with the list as you will."

"Why are you helping me?"

"Don't ask me why, but my mother would be heart-sick if you lost this ramshackle place."

"That's your mother's reason. What's yours?"

"I love my mother. I want what she wants. Simple as that."

"I don't know what to say."

"Say thank you."

"Thank you, Asa, from the bottom of my heart."

"Just one more thing."

"What's that?"

"You hurt my mother, I'll kill you."

36

I was at Wickliffe Manor helping Franklin wash over one hundred glasses, souvenirs from the most exciting two minutes in sports—the Kentucky Derby.

It was the least I could do for Hunter after Asa's appalling behavior.

Yes, Hunter told me.

It's not every day the daughter of a man's girlfriend threatens him if he misbehaves. There was no point in contacting Asa and persuading her to apologize. After all, she was saving the Wickliffe farm.

My thought was that Asa was getting Franklin and Hunter out of a bind, so they should take a little vinegar with the sugar. She was what she was.

Franklin and I put the glasses upside down on towels and carefully went through them—sorting, evaluating, and drying.

Out of one hundred and thirteen glasses, we had twenty-eight doubles, five cracked, and seven chipped.

Franklin took out the cracked and chipped glasses,

leaving one hundred and one Kentucky Derby glasses to price, catalog, and photograph.

The Derby Glass tradition started in 1938 with a souvenir water glass. It was only in 1939 the Kentucky Derby Festival Association started their weeklong celebration of the Kentucky Derby by issuing true Mint Julep glasses—a 12 oz. glass that stood 5 ¼ inches tall with a 2 ¾ inch diameter.

In 1945 a tall glass that stood 6 inches high was commissioned as well. The 1945 "tall" glass was incredibly rare, but Franklin happened to have one sitting on his dining room table.

I booted up Franklin's laptop and searched for the "tall" Derby glass on the internet. "Franklin, this one glass alone is worth over three hundred dollars."

"Let's keep going. We have the Bakelite sets from 1941 to 1944."

"Any aluminum WWII glasses?"

"One."

"The prices are all over the place. I see some being sold for five hundred dollars and others at six thousand. I have no idea what makes the difference."

"I think we should sell these glasses as a lot. It's going to take time and effort to sell them individually."

"Who collected them?" I asked.

"I guess my great-grandfather started collecting them. My mother used them for Derby parties on the Friday night before the big race."

"Your family threw Derby parties?"

"Every year. The next morning we'd pile into a limousine and head to Churchill Downs to watch the race with our parents and their friends in a private box."

"Wow! When was the last time you did that?"

"It must have been early teens or so, right around then. We stopped when Mother became ill."

"Is that when things began to fall apart?"

"Hunter was gone, and Mother relied on me. Dad did the best he could, but running both the farm and his practice while taking care of Mother was too much. I tried to help, but I was just a kid. There wasn't much I could do besides mow the pastures and keep Mom company. Those were dreadful years."

"Did Hunter know the extent of your mother's illness?"

"I don't think so. After Mother's funeral, he and Dad got into a big argument. I remember Hunter storming out of the house. We didn't see much of him after Mom's death. It wasn't long before he left for London."

"Hmm."

"What are you thinking, Jo?"

"Hey, guys, how are the glasses doing?" Hunter asked, coming into the dining room.

"I think you have a little cash cow here," I answered, smiling.

Hunter, as usual, looked sexy in a white shirt with

the sleeves rolled up. It showed off his farmer's tan rather nicely.

"Great. I'll start photographing."

"What else can I do?" I asked.

"I'm still trying to find documentation about the rifle. Can you and Franklin search for anything that might be of value? Letters, bills of sale, autographs."

"Where do you want us to start?" Franklin asked, getting a bottle of water out of the fridge. He offered me one, but I shook my head no.

"Start in Mother's bedroom. We'll go from there."

"Okay," Franklin said, trudging up the back stairwell.

I went around to the rickety elevator and prayed it still worked. Last time I was in it, the poor thing gasped and sputtered as though giving me its last breath.

When I entered the bedroom, Franklin was already pulling boxes out of his mother's closet.

I had never been in Mrs. Wickliffe's room before but it shouted feminine. The walls were covered in vintage rose pattern wallpaper, which was yellowing. The four-poster bed was the standard dark, heavy carved furniture of the nineteenth century, but the delicate bedcover matched the frilly white curtains. The fireplace mantel held pictures of Hunter and Franklin in sterling frames.

Her makeup vanity was classic forties with the round mirror and looked out of place, but I got the feeling the vanity had been her mother's and posed a personal connection for Mrs. Wickliffe. Bottles of perfume and silver hairbrushes lay as though recently placed by loving hands.

Franklin and I were in a ghost room, and I was not sure we had the right to go through his mother's private effects.

A picture of Mrs. Wickliffe on her wedding day stood on the nightstand. She looked stunning with dark hair and eyes, her face glowing with happiness. Her marriage to Hunter and Franklin's father was obviously a love match, and I could see Hunter got his good looks from her.

Picking up the frame, I wiped the dust off. The room was disquieting. As I watched Franklin pull out boxes, I discerned the closets still contained his mother's clothes. This wasn't a bedroom. It was a shrine, and obviously, neither man had recovered from their mother's death.

"Franklin, why are we going through your mother's things? I hardly think we will find a bill of sale for an old gun in your mother's private papers."

"It's sad to say this about one's own mother, but Mom was a packrat. She loved paper. The storage area under the main stairs has every assignment Hunter and I did for school. I mean, every drawing, every test, and every project. Even doodling. She would get scraps out of our wastebaskets and save them."

"Hand me a box then."

Franklin brought over a cardboard box, and I dumped the contents onto the bed. Franklin did likewise on the floor. We spent the next several hours going through old Christmas cards, baking recipes, utility receipts, and notes to the cleaning lady until Hunter yelled up the stairway, "Are you guys done? I'm finished with the photographing. How about some lunch?"

I yelled back, "We've got two more boxes. Can you wait?"

"Yeah."

Franklin stood up and stretched. "I want to take a break. We can do this after lunch."

"You go on, Franklin. I'm going to finish. Can you bring those two boxes over to me before you leave?"

Franklin dumped the boxes on the bed. "Don't take too much time."

"Go ahead and start lunch without me. I shan't be long. Just a quick look-see."

"Okey-dokey. See ya in a few."

Most of the contents from the boxes consisted of personal letters tied with ribbons. I quickly looked at the return addresses on the letters. Most of them were from friends vacationing in exotic ports of call. I doubted one of them would hold the bill of sale for the rifle.

I was hastily putting the stacks of letters back into

the box when I came across a small canvas rolled up and tied with a purple ribbon.

Cutting the ribbon with scissors I found in the nightstand, I unrolled the canvas and spread the painting on the bed. It was a landscape of a waterfall in a mountainous setting. I sniffed the paint and felt the texture. It smelled musty, but was definitely an oil painting. Turning it over, I searched the back for the signature, then flipped it over and searched again on the front.

In the diffused light coming through the filmy curtains, I located the artist's signature. Leaning against the headboard, I closed my eyes. A faint breeze drifted across my face, which was impossible as the windows were closed. "Mrs. Wickliffe," I whispered, "did you suspect this dire day would come, and you put back something that would help your boys?"

I waited for an answer, and after receiving none, I picked up the canvas and went downstairs.

37

Hunter had set a plate at the kitchen table for me. "Wash your hands," he said cheerfully.

"Look, Jo," Franklin said. "The chef has prepared peanut butter and jelly sandwiches."

"Only the best for my family," Hunter teased as he filled my water glass.

"May I have some bourbon, please? I need something stronger."

Franklin and Hunter exchanged glances.

"I can fix you something else," Hunter suggested.

"No. No. Peanut butter is fine."

Hunter asked, "Is there a problem?"

"The exact opposite," I said, laying the canvas on the table.

"What's this?" Franklin inquired, picking up the canvas.

"Franklin, don't get any jelly on it, please," I begged.

"What's the big deal? It's just an old painting Mother was fond of."

"I remember it," Hunter said, running his fingers

over the impasto texture of the painting. "Mother said she was putting it away for a rainy day. She was afraid Father would give it to one of his no-account relatives who admired it."

"Wonder what Mother meant," Franklin mused. "I had forgotten about it."

"I'm so glad I'm an art historian. Otherwise, you two would be up a creek. Look at the signature, guys."

Both Franklin and Hunter peered at the signature.

"Yeah?" asked Franklin, mystified.

"Thomas Cole was a landscape artist who founded the Hudson River School and influenced nineteenth-century landscape painting. Forget about the rifle, boys. If this painting checks out, not only will the estate be saved, but you'll be able to buy several Rolls-Royces, Hunter."

"Are you sure?" Hunter asked, dumbfounded.

"Ninety percent sure. You need to provide the provenance, but I'm sure it's an original Thomas Cole. Just needs an appraiser's authentication."

Hunter picked me up and swung me around, while Franklin did the moonwalk around the kitchen.

"Bourbon? Hell, let's get out the champagne!" Franklin yelled. "Whoopee! We're not the ginger-headed stepchildren anymore." He ran over and hugged both of us.

I didn't even mind being squashed between the two of them.

Well, not much.

38

Shaneika and I were having lunch downtown when we spied Detective Drake passing in an unmarked police car. I stared after it for a moment contemplating where he was headed then went back to eating my pasta salad.

"I heard some police scuttlebutt about the Gage Cagle case the other day," Shaneika offered.

"You have a mole in the department?"

"It always helps to have friends."

"Listening."

"All charges have been dropped against your friend, Rosamond Rose."

"Why's that?"

"The weapon she supposedly dropped does not fit Gage's wound forensically."

"Huh."

"There is a possibility Willow Cherry or Eli Owsley murdered Gage because Gage bungled the sale of the Porter Clay chairs. The DA doesn't feel a case against Rosamond is winnable. There's not enough evidence."

"What did Rosie drop?"

"A sharp woodworking tool, but not the one that killed Cagle."

"It had blood on it."

"Could have been she saw it on the floor and picked it up when she found Cagle. People do that all the time. You have no idea how many innocent people are discovered with the murder weapon in their hands because they either pulled it out of the victim or picked it up."

"*North by Northwest.*"

"What does an old Alfred Hitchcock movie have to do with Cagle?"

"Cary Grant pulls a knife out of a man in front of dozens of witnesses. It was a setup."

"Are you saying Rosie was framed?"

I didn't reply. Perhaps Shaneika was right that Rosie was dealt a rotten hand.

I picked at my salad, thinking about Shaneika's news, but I couldn't shake the feeling Rosie was involved. After all, I didn't see what she was holding in the other hand.

Of course, I'm paranoid. After my ordeal with my "friend" Sandy Sloan, who tried to kill me, I have a healthy distrust of friends.

Every person is capable of murder if pushed hard enough.

Even sweet, unassuming Rosamond Rose.

Even me.

39

I got a call.

"Come running," was all Bess said.

Since I had returned my borrowed golf cart to Charles, I drove my Prius to the Big House, wondering what needed my attention so urgently.

A van blocked the entrance to the front door, which is just as well, as I always go through the kitchen door. I drove to the back of the house and hurried into the kitchen.

"Hello. Hello. Where is everyone?" No one was in the kitchen. I popped my head into Charles' office. No one. I moseyed into the foyer. The front door was wide open with workmen scurrying back and forth.

I followed them into the library where June, Charles, Bess, and Amelia were seated.

On the floor was spread a large tarpaulin with the two comb-back Windsor chairs sitting on top.

"Jumping Jehoshaphat! What are those chairs doing here?"

A small bald man stepped into the room with a briefcase that looked more like a toolkit. "I can explain. You must be Asa Reynolds' mother, Mrs. Reynolds."

"What does my daughter have to do with any of this?"

June chirped, "Asa bought those chairs for me. It appears Eli Owsley is selling everything he owns to pay his high-priced lawyer."

"But why these chairs? They're fakes."

"Not necessarily. Please let me explain, Mrs. Reynolds. My name is Benjamin Quick. I consult for the Speed Museum in Louisville. As you know, they have a large collection of eighteenth and nineteenth-century Kentucky-made furniture. Your daughter hired me to authenticate the furniture she has purchased and is donating to Lady Elsmere's future museum."

Mr. Quick was wearing a three-piece black suit with a watch chain and fob hanging from his vest pocket. His glasses were round with no rims. He was so closely shaved, the skin on his face glistened from the use of lye soap and a razor—straight-edged, no doubt.

"Mr. Quick is an expert on American-made furniture from 1700 to 1840," Charles claimed.

"Once the Industrial Revolution comes into play, I lose interest. I'm afraid I'm very old school. Mass production holds no appeal for me."

June beamed at Mr. Quick. "You're among friends."

"Shall we get started?" Mr. Quick asked, rubbing his

hands in anticipation.

Bess jumped up with her phone to record the appraisal. "You don't mind, do you?"

Mr. Quick joked, "If I had known I was going to be filmed for posterity, I would have worn my blue serge suit. Shows off my baby blues to perfection."

I sat next to June to watch Mr. Quick. He smelled, licked, and felt the wood on both chairs. Turning them upside down, he inspected the wood, paying special attention to the joints and seat.

"It's very unusual to find these writing chairs without any repairs and all spindles intact. These must have been beloved."

"Or they could be fakes," I chimed in.

June nudged me, giving me a dirty look.

Ooh, a double whammy of disapproval.

Mr. Quick sat in both chairs before he pulled out the four quill drawers to check the dovetail corners. He sniffed the wood and ran his fingernail around the top of the drawers. "Beeswax is coating the inside of the drawers."

Next, he pulled out a tool resembling a surgeon's scalpel and scraped a minute amount of paint from the backside of each chair, taking the samples over to a table set up with a microscope.

With phone in hand, Bess followed Mr. Quick religiously, darting about him like a nervous fly.

"Uh-huh," Mr. Quick mumbled.

"What did he say?" June asked.

"Nothing important," I answered.

For someone who stated he was uninterested in the idea of a museum, Charles was sitting on the edge of his chair, tapping his fingers on the end table next to him.

Mr. Quick took an envelope from his pocket. "Ladies and gentleman, this is a sealed letter from Asa Reynolds. She requested I open it after the paint had been tested. Miss Bess, will you verify this letter is sealed and addressed to me?"

Delighted to be included in the appraisal, Bess handed the phone to her sister, Amelia, to continue filming. "Yes, Mr. Quick, the letter is sealed."

Mr. Quick handed Bess the letter. "Has the letter been tampered with?"

"Not that I can tell," replied Bess, looking at the camera.

"Is that a no?"

"Yes, I mean no. It shows no signs of tampering."

"Would you please open the letter?"

Bess tore open the envelope with great enthusiasm and took out a letter, handing it to Mr. Quick.

With a curious expression on his face, Mr. Quick quickly read the letter then handed it to Bess. "Please read aloud."

Mr. Quick,

You have undoubtedly tested the paint and have come to the same conclusion I have made about the chairs. So there is no doubt as to their authenticity, please check the screws from the locks in the top quill drawers.

I have taken the liberty of testing one drawer, but you will find the lock on the other drawer undisturbed.

Thank you. Asa Reynolds

Mr. Quick hummed as he rummaged through his small case of tools and picked out a small screwdriver. "Lady Elsmere, I'm going to have to dismantle the locks, dear lady."

"Do what you have to do, sir."

"Very good then," Mr. Quick said as he took both drawers over to his worktable. With deft movements, Mr. Quick dismantled one lock, took out the screws, and photographed them. Then he placed the screws on a magnetic plate under his microscope. "Mmmm."

"What's he mumbling?" June asked.

"Nothing important," I hissed. Like Charles, I was now caught up in the excitement.

Quietly, Mr. Quick reassembled the lock on the quill drawer, putting it back in the rightful chair. He repeated the same procedure with the second chair, reassembling the drawer when finished.

Sitting at the work desk, Mr. Quick made copious notes on his laptop, proofread what he had written, and snapped the computer shut.

The rest of us jumped at the sound.

Mr. Quick stood, tugging on his vest before buttoning his jacket. He strode over and stopped, looming over our little group. "Lady Elsmere and friends. Let's start with the supposed bill of sale from Porter Clay to Roald Jansen for a bedstead and other furniture. While there is no specific mention of the Windsor chairs, the bill of sale is authentic. Both signatures have been verified as true.

"I did track down a descendant of Mr. Jansen's who sent me pictures of family members sitting in the chairs dating from the twentieth century. After 1989, the chairs were kept in storage until they were consigned to Mr. Owsley when the family farm was sold. I have a copy of the agreement with Mr. Owsley, so the provenance has been established without a doubt."

June started to interrupt, but Mr. Quick held up his hand. "Please let me finish, Lady Elsmere. Thank you."

He looked at some notes in his hands before continuing. "The wood used in the construction is wood that could be procured locally and was typically used by Kentucky furniture makers. The condition of the joints, along with the nicks, scratches, and general wear and tear are consistent, but the remarkable condition of the chairs gave me pause. There are no signs of repairs. All the spindles are intact. Very rare for chairs this old, but not impossible if the chairs were well cared for.

"The next item I checked was the paint. A casual observer viewing the chairs would believe they were painted black. However, they were originally painted a bright green that we call verdigris, which is a mixture of various copper acetates and linseed oil. Over time, photooxidation occurs, and the paint darkens to brown and then black. In other words, sunlight and oxygen break down the paint. I believe the paint contains copper and linseed oil, but spectral analysis in the lab should verify my conclusions.

"Next, following Ms. Reynolds' instructions, I looked at the screws for the locks. This is where most forgers make a mistake. They use modern screws made to look old, but in the eighteenth century, furniture makers made their screws from hand-forged blanks, so each screw varies in shape and thread pitch, making each screw unique. I checked all eight screws, and all eight are unique unto themselves.

"Lady Elsmere, I can say without a doubt, the Jansen chairs are authentic Kentucky-made furniture, fashioned anywhere from 1780 to 1820. I will have all my conclusions double-checked by my colleagues at the Speed Museum once the lab test findings come back, but I'd say you have the real McCoy."

June asked, "What about Porter Clay?"

"The carving of the letters PC, 1799 caused some concern as we have not found carving of initials or dates on any other furniture made by Porter Clay, but it would not be unheard of if Roald Jansen carved the initials and date himself, being proud of having such handsome furniture in his home.

"Once the tests verify my findings, we can say the chairs are *attributed* to Porter Clay. That's the best we can do until further documentation is discovered." Mr. Quick pulled out his gold pocket watch and looked at the time. "You must excuse me, but I have an appointment in Cincinnati and must scoot."

June stood and shook his hand, as did Charles and the rest of the group, including myself. "Thank you so much. We all appreciate your help in this matter."

"It was nothing. I am excited to be part of such a find. I hope, Lady Elsmere, you will be generous enough to loan these chairs to the Speed Museum for a future exhibit."

June smiled and asked Charles to help with Mr. Quick's equipment and show him out. It wasn't lost on anyone that she didn't answer his request about loaning the furniture.

June, Bess, and Amelia clustered around the chairs while I picked up the letter Asa had written.

It was, indeed, in Asa's sprawling, cursive handwriting. On the bottom she had added a postscript:

See, Mother, I really am an insurance investigator. Only this time, the seller was the fraud, not the furniture.

40

The fact that the Porter Clay chairs were the real deal threw an entirely new light on Gage Cagle's death. There was also the news Eli Owsley had recanted his confession, and the plea deal was off the table.

Why were Eli, Willow, and Gage arguing?

Let's say Eli knew Gage and June didn't get along so he encouraged Gage to help him run up the price of the chairs by bidding against June. As the gallery owner, Eli Owsley would have earned a hefty commission on the chairs, and would have been furious with Gage for spoiling the sale, but Willow Cherry didn't have a dog in that fight. Why had Willow been angry?

Perhaps Eli hadn't asked Gage to come to the auction. Maybe Gage showed up and took it upon himself to engage in a bidding war.

Perhaps many of the forged pieces that Willow Cherry made were auctioned that night. Gage's appearance likely caused sales to be lower than anticipated because of the turmoil that followed Gage wherever he went. Very few people liked Gage except misogynistic, mean-spirited old farts like himself.

That still wouldn't explain why Eli or Willow would murder Gage. Willow was making the forgeries on Gage's property, and Gage was keeping a keen eye on the property, creating an isolated and safe environment—the perfect haven for their illegal activities. It didn't make sense for either one of them to kill Gage. He was the one enabling all three of them to make money.

But Eli would have reason to kill Willow if he believed Willow had murdered Gage, thinking he might be next. The reason why Willow might kill Gage didn't matter. Eli thought he had better get Willow before Willow got him. Shoot first and ask questions later.

There was only one person who stood to benefit from Gage's death, and that person was Rosie.

Ring around the rosie,
Pocket full of posies,
Ashes! Ashes!
We all fall down.

41

I wasn't specifically thinking of the Black Plague when I knocked on Rosie's door, but I was thinking of death.

Rosie answered the door with a dishrag in her hand while her dogs caused a ruckus in the background.

"Josiah, this is unexpected. I haven't seen you since the auction."

There was a little bit of anger and accusation in her voice, but I let it pass.

"I want you to leave town."

"What?"

"You heard me. Get out of town."

"You're talking crazy."

"I know you killed Gage, and I'm not spending the next few years looking over my shoulder wondering when you're coming after me, so you've gotta get gone."

"The charges against me have been dropped. I'm off the hook," Rosie protested.

"Eli Owsley tore up his plea deal, and if he wins his

case, the police are going to be looking for a new fall guy. They're going to be knocking on your door again, Rosie."

"There's no evidence tying me to Gage's case."

"There's me."

Rosie's expression hardened. "Josiah, I tell you, I didn't kill the man."

"I heard a thump, which was Gage falling after you stabbed him. I saw you standing over his body with blood smeared on your dress."

"Exactly. Not blood splatter. You forget, Josiah, that the object I dropped was not the weapon that killed the old man. Cutting his femoral artery would have caused blood to spurt like a fountain."

"I've thought about it. The reason there was no blood splatter was because you were pressed up against him when you stabbed him, and your dress caught the initial spurt of blood. Your dress soaked it up like a sponge. I saw you. You were covered in his blood."

Rosie seemed momentarily taken aback, but quickly recovered her composure. "I heard him fall and reached him before you did. I was trying to help."

"You were watching Gage bleed out."

"I went for help."

"You ran away, probably to hide the real weapon you used on him. I think you picked up whatever sharp object you could find in the storage room. There were old tools and knives lying around everywhere so you had plenty to choose from. You used two objects to strike at Gage simultaneously, and one did the job for you. When you saw me, you dropped the ineffectual weapon and ran to hide the deadly one, which you hid in the folds of your dress. If the police were to search the grounds of the auction house again or conduct a search here, would they find something?"

Rosie studied me quietly before speaking, "You have nothing to fear from me."

"Yes, I do. The fact that I can finger you will make you sweat at night, and sooner or later, you'll come for me. But remember, Rosie, if you take me on, you take on Asa, and you'll never escape her. The only way out of this mess is for you to leave so I don't have to worry. You hightail it out of Kentucky as far as you can get, and I suddenly have a lapse of memory. Capiche?"

Rosie licked her lips. "Gage had it coming, Josiah."

"I never said he didn't, Rosie. I'm just saying I don't want to suffer the same fate."

One of Rosie's dogs was yapping around her ankles, and she leaned over to quiet it. When turning to face me again, she had an oddly serene smile on her face. "I'll study on your words."

"I'd better never see you again, but I wish you well wherever you go. You got a raw deal, Rosie."

Rosie shut her door, and I hurried to my car.

What have I told you repeatedly about Kentucky being a "dark and bloody ground!" It even turns saints into sinners.

EPILOGUE

I was having a celebration dinner with Hunter after his triumphant return from New York. Both brothers had taken their mother's painting to New York for the auction. The Thomas Cole painting sold for enough money to pay off all Hunter's debts and keep both him and Franklin solvent for many years to come.

While Hunter hurried home to me, Franklin stayed in New York several days longer to eat, drink, and be merry, throwing off a year of terrible strain.

"What happened while I was gone?" Hunter asked, pouring wine into my glass.

"June's museum project is on, and she and Charles are discussing where to build it."

"You mean arguing?"

"That's how they discuss things. June wants a new building on the outskirts of town, but Charles wants to refurbish a tobacco warehouse in a not-so-nice district."

"I'm with Charles on this one."

"Don't confess that to June, or you'll never be summoned to dinner again."

"I understand Rosamond Rose sold her house and is moving to the West Coast."

"June bought it and Gage's property as well. She's going to give it to Charles as a Christmas present with the stipulation he can never sell her Thoroughbreds after her death, but give them a permanent home on Gage's farm after they retire from racing."

"I wish all horsemen in the racing business treated their horses with the same consideration."

"Hear! Hear!" I said, raising my glass. "Enough about June. Let's toast to your success."

"I owe much to Asa."

"You would have found your way eventually. Asa just sped up the process."

Hunter lifted his glass as well. "Here's to a happy and healthy life for both of us."

"I'll drink to that." I laughed while clinking his glass.

We had a lovely dinner at Wickliffe Manor, watched an old movie, and fell asleep. I woke up early and left Hunter snoring on the couch, but not before I slipped a letter on the coffee table addressed to him from his mother, written days before she died. I had discovered it when going through her papers. She had meant it to be read with the discovery of the painting, but I knew Hunter was not ready to read it then.

"Mrs. Wickliffe, I did as you wanted," I whispered. "Go into the light. Both boys are fine. Your job is done."

A soft sigh winged down the massive stairway and passed my face out the front door.

I followed.

The information concerning Madame du Berry's chairs, early Kentucky furniture, derby glasses, antiques in general, and forgeries is correct. Porter Clay, John Bonewitz, Thomas Cole, and Ann Bateman were real people and accomplished artists in their respective fields. I don't claim to be an expert, but found antiques to be a fascinating research subject and am now a fan. I look at old furniture in a different light. Each piece of handmade furniture has a life and a history all its own—a time capsule that speaks to us if we understand its language.

I love to learn new things. Don't you?

Like to receive special offers?
Feel free to sign up for my newsletter at
www.abigailkeam.com.

Did you like Death By Stalking?
Please leave a review at place of purchase.
Thank you.

Read On For More Exciting Bonus Chapters

1

Veritas Noble and I had just seen the classic *The Apartment* with Jack Lemon and Shirley MacLaine at the Kentucky Theater and were heading back to her car when she exclaimed, "Oh, Josiah. Someone has run into my Subaru Impreza!"

We both rushed and surveyed the damage to the back of her bumper which someone had severely dented.

"That's terrible," I said, looking around for cars whose color matched the paint marks scratched on the bumper. "Wait a minute, VeVe," I said, referring to my nickname for her, as Veritas was too much of a mouthful. "There's an envelope under the windshield wiper."

Veritas pulled a white envelope out from the wiper and tore it open. It contained a large wad of cash. "Josiah, there's a thousand dollars here," she said, incredulously.

"Read the note."

Pulling out a handwritten note she read—"*'I'm sorry. Hope this helps.'* Just when I thought the worst, I find this. Kind of restores my faith in humanity. My insurance has such a high deductible."

"Do you think the money will cover the cost of fixing the bumper?"

"It should be close enough. I feel so much better now."

"It was very nice to leave some money, but who walks around with a thousand bucks in his pocket?" I wondered out loud.

"I don't know and don't care. Let's go. I want to get home."

"Can you get my packages out of the trunk?"

"Yeah. Looks like the trunk wasn't affected," Veritas said, inserting her key and opening it.

How shall I put this? The trunk swung open. We both stared at its contents, gasped, and ran down the street screaming.

A dead man had been stuffed into Veritas' trunk.

2

Let me introduce myself. My name is Josiah Louise Reynolds. My grandmother named me after a righteous Hebrew king. I'm anything but. I'm not a king and definitely not righteous. I live on a farm near the Palisades in the Bluegrass overlooking the Kentucky River. I raise honey bees and make my living selling honey at the local farmers' market, boarding horses, and renting out my iconic home, the Butterfly, for events like wedding receptions.

I'm in my fifties, wear a hearing aid, walk with a slight limp, and in pain much of the time, although the pain has lessened. I am mannerly, housebroken, and presentable in public without embarrassing myself or others—most of the time.

That takes care of me.

As for Veritas, she is an old friend, and we had spent an enjoyable evening together until we opened the trunk of her car.

We ran screeching pell-mell, coming to a halt only

when I careened into a parked car. I grabbed hold of Veritas' jacket. "Stop, VeVe. I can't go on."

"I think I peed on myself," Veritas said, glumly.

"You're not the only one who needs to change her panties. Come on. Let's see about this."

"No."

"The man might need assistance."

"He looked dead to me, Josiah."

"Stay here, then. If someone is playing a gag, and that stiff jumps out at me, I'm gonna make sure he's dead."

I made my way back to the car parked behind the theater. The trunk was still open, and the street was eerily quiet as if nothing untoward had happened. Peering cautiously into the trunk, I sputtered, "Sir, are you all right?"

I inched closer still and poked him with a finger. The man's head lolled to where I could see his face. He was dead all right. His eyes stared up at me with that blank look that only the dead have. I should know since I've stumbled upon my share of lifeless bodies during the past few years.

Digging into my purse, I pulled out my phone and used its itty bitty light to get a better look inside the trunk. The unfortunate man was a white male with nice features who must have been handsome in life. He was thirtyish, wearing expensive blue jeans, posh tennis shoes, black tee shirt, and jacket. His hair had been cut recently, and his nails appeared to be professionally manicured. Rigor mortis had not set in yet, which meant the man had died within the last three hours. My concentration was broken by the clip-clop of Veritas' approaching steps.

"Is he?" Veritas asked.

"Sure looks like it."

"How did he die?"

"Don't know but there's a small blood pool underneath him. Better get the police, VeVe. I'll stay here with the body while you go."

"I'll be back in a jiffy," Veritas said, quickly walking to the police station only a block away.

I took the opportunity of her absence to rifle through the man's pockets and go through his wallet. I switched on my phone's camera, taking pictures of both the body, possessions, and the dented bumper before the police arrived. I even took a small paint sample from the scratching on the bumper and dropped it into an empty pill bottle in my purse. Seconds later, a squad car with two uniforms pulled up with Veritas riding in the back. I turned with a frightened, panicky look plastered on my face for the benefit of the male policemen who expected such scared looks from women after stuffing my phone in my pocket. Who am I to stand in the way of archaic prejudices?

A beat cop nudged me aside and felt for a pulse. "Yep, he's dead." He eyed us suspiciously. "Touch anything?"

"Why no, Officer," I lied. "Why would we do that?"

"Did you know him?"

Both Veritas and I shook our heads.

"Whose car is this?"

"Mine," Veritas said, her voice quaking a bit.

"We'll need you both to make a statement. This officer will show you to police headquarters."

"Don't bother. I know the way. Come on, VeVe. Let's get this over with."

"What a horrible evening," Veritas said, peering over her shoulder at the cop following us to the police station.

I couldn't have agreed more.

3

Norbet Drake walked into the interrogation room with a Styrofoam coffee cup in one hand and a file in the other. He glanced at me, shaking his head. "You are certainly a bad penny. How do you manage to keep any friends when bodies keep piling up around you? I would give you a wide berth."

"Nice to see you too, Norbet."

He sighed, "It's Detective Drake."

"We see each other so often, I thought we should be on a first name basis."

"It's rather like a revolving door for you and this police station. Okay, Josiah, let's hear your story this time."

"May I call you Norbet?"

"No."

"Then it's Mrs. Reynolds." I batted my eyelashes.

"Do you always act like this just to be difficult?"

"Hmm, yeah, I think I do."

Detective Drake cleared his throat. "Let's get on

with this." He clicked on the video recorder. "It is twenty-two hundred hours on Sunday—."

I interrupted. "He must have been shot."

Detective Drake looked up from his file. "What makes you say so?"

"Because you made VeVe and me take a GSR test. Who does that anymore? It's a rather outdated test, isn't it?"

"When you say VeVe, do you mean Veritas Noble?"

"Did you know Veritas was the Roman goddess of truth? VeVe, that's what I call her, is very much like her namesake. I don't think she's ever told a lie in her life. I don't think she even can. If VeVe says something, you can take it to the bank."

"For this interview, let's refer to VeVe as Veritas Noble."

"Okay, but let's get back to the gunshot residue test."

"Mrs. Reynolds, I was under the impression I am conducting this interview."

"Interview? See, that's the problem. I thought we were merely giving statements as witnesses to discovering a body. My being interviewed means you think I'm a suspect. Did you find gunshot residue on my hands?"

Detective Drake leaned back in his chair. "NO! We didn't."

"So, I'm not a suspect?"

"My mouth waters at the thought."

"Did you find a gun on me, VeVe, or in her car?"

"Privileged information."

I replied, "Which means no. Did you find a gun anywhere in or near the crime scene like a dumpster or a storm drain?"

Detective Drake crossed his arms while clenching his jaw muscles.

I said, "I think the perpetrator took his gun with him."

"What do you think happened?"

"I haven't a clue. You're the detective," I replied in my best helpless female tone of voice.

"Will we find your DNA on the victim's body?"

"You will. I touched him to see if there was a pulse."

"What about Veritas Noble?"

"After opening the trunk, she never got close to the body again."

"Why did Mrs. Noble open the trunk?"

"I asked her. We had been shopping before the movie, and I wanted to get my packages from the trunk since we were going home."

"Why not leave them in the trunk?"

"It would save VeVe getting out of the car again when she dropped me off at home."

"What did you do when you saw the body?"

"We both ran away. I believe I was screaming. I think VeVe was, too. I ran headlong into another car. A bruise has formed on my leg. Would you like to see it?"

Detective Drake ignored my suggestion to see the bruise.

It used to be when I teased a man about showing part of my anatomy, he jumped at the chance. Now, men acted as if a bee had stung them. It's tough getting old, girls.

Drake asked, "Did you know the suspect?"

"It was dark and the man's face was turned away," I replied, trying to stifle a yawn.

Drake checked the report in the file. "The man's face was facing up when the officer arrived."

"Yes, only because I checked for a pulse."

"Did Mrs. Noble know him?"

"You'll have to ask her."

"Why did you park behind the theater instead of Main Street?"

"We went to see a movie and all the parking spaces were taken on Main Street, so we parked in the back."

"Why not use the parking garage half a block over?"

"Women dislike using parking garages."

"Even if it is attached to a police station?"

"We parked only a block from the police station and look what happened right under your noses. A man was murdered and thrown into the trunk of a woman's car."

"Okay, I've had enough. We'll call you back in if we need something further."

"You will talk to my lawyer, Shaneika Mary Todd, if you need something further. I gave your men a statement. I complied with your GSR test. I'm done talking. See ya around, Norbet." I gave Detective Drake a big smile, relieved the police hadn't searched me. For if they had, they would have found gloves tucked in my pants' pocket. Otherwise, my prints would have been discovered all over that dead man.

I may be a snoop, but that is no reason to make the police think I'm a killer.

4

A loud knocking at the door woke me up. Since Baby, my English Mastiff, wasn't growling, it must be someone he knew, and he didn't know anyone I didn't know. I pushed off the cat sleeping on my chest, and tried avoiding stepping on other felines from the Kitty Kaboodle, the clowder of barn cats, which were Baby's pets and let in every night. Two were curled around Baby still sleeping. One was on my dressing table, knocking off lipstick tubes. Another was climbing up the draperies.

I hurried to the front door and opened it. "Morning, Charles," I said to Lady Elsmere's heir. He was also her butler and estate manager. In other words, he was the big cheese at the Big House. "What can I do for you?"

"Good morning, Josiah. Her Ladyship would like a word with you."

"Now?"

"Right now."

"You woke me up."

"Please don't make me go back without you."

Seeing Charles' distressed expression, I assumed Lady Elsmere, aka June Webster from Monkey's Eyebrow, Kentucky was on the warpath about something. Probably one of my peacocks had pooped on her patio again. "Give me a minute to get dressed."

"Please hurry."

"Can I at least brush my hair and maybe my teeth?"

"If you must."

"Gee, thanks. Come on in. Help yourself to the fridge while I dress."

"Thanks, Josiah."

"Know what it is about?"

"Rather not say."

"Is it serious? Should I call a lawyer?" I teased.

"Nothing like that. I'll wait in the car until you get ready."

"Okay, be out in a jiffy." I hurried to my room, brushed my teeth, splashed water on my face, and threw on some clothes. I stumbled over Baby who had moved from my bedside to the front of the bathroom door. Mastiffs like to lie in doorways. "Good golly, Baby. You trying to kill me or somethin'? If I die, who is going feed you?"

Baby raised his massive head, yawned, and replaced his drooping jowls upon his paws, seemingly unconcerned by my threat.

After finding some flip-flops under a chair, I hurried out to the Bentley waiting for me. Ooh, June sent the important car to fetch me. Must be serious.

We arrived at the Big House, and Charles dropped me off at the back entrance. "Yoo-hoo," I called, striding into a large kitchen.

At the kitchen table sat Bess, Charles' daughter and cook extraordinaire, Amelia, another daughter and June's caretaker, and finally, June, the great lady herself.

June held up a newspaper. "What's this, and you didn't even bother to tell me?"

I grabbed the paper from June and read the front page. There was a large article about Veritas and me finding the body.

"What is it with you and dead bodies? It's becoming a filthy habit."

I replied, "I know. I know. They seem to be piling up, don't they?"

"One or two dead people is one thing, but there's been over a dozen in the past few years. It's unseemly and people are starting to talk."

"Starting to? Tongues have been wagging ever since Brannon left me for that skank half his age."

Ignoring the reference to my late husband's mistress, Ellen Boudreaux, June asked, "Why was I kept out of the loop?"

"It just happened last night, June. I got home late and went to bed. I haven't had time to tell anyone, let alone you."

Bess said, "I made a chocolate mousse cake for tonight, but you can have a piece if you spill. We want the skinny from the horse's mouth."

I sat down. "Breakfast it is then. I'll take one of your bribes anytime, Bess."

Bess jumped up and served a huge piece of chocolate deliciousness along with a glass of milk. Now, that's what I call a good breakfast. Sugar and chocolate. Better than caffeine to get a body going.

Amelia said, "It says a young man was found in the trunk of Veritas Noble's car."

"True," I replied, taking a big bite out of the cake. "His name was Shelby Carpenter."

"The newspaper article said the police weren't releasing the name of the victim until the family was notified," Amelia said.

"I'm nothing if not resourceful, Bess. I have my ways." I wasn't about to admit that I had sifted through the man's wallet, even to Lady Elsmere and her peeps.

"Shelby Carpenter. Shelby Carpenter," Bess mused thoughtfully. "Wasn't that the name of a character played by Vincent Price in the movie *Laura?*

"I didn't know you like old movies," I said.

"Who was the victim?" June asked, ignoring Bess.

"I looked him up on the Internet. He was a freelance reporter," I answered.

"What does that mean?" June asked before taking a

sip of her coffee.

I replied, "I gather he investigated stories on his own and wrote about them on his blog. Sometimes a newspaper would pick an article up. His blog had over six hundred thousand followers."

"Impressive," Bess said. "Where was he based?"

"Washington, DC."

June asked, "So he wrote about politics."

"A lot of the time, but anything that interested him I guess."

"If he was an investigative reporter, what was he doing here?" Amelia asked.

I said, "Better yet, who didn't want him to nose around the Bluegrass and was willing to kill him over it? Heard anything through the grapevine, June? You always have sources who feed you information."

"Ah, fiddle de de. Nothing but the scuttlebutt on Ferrina Landau's party to show off her new necklace bought by her doddering old fool of a husband."

Bess mused, "Is Ferrina one of those made-up names for white girls?"

"Everything about the woman is made-up from her pumped-up lips to her reconstructed bum."

"Easy there, June. People might think you don't like her," I chided, smiling. I loved it when June brandished her claws. "I take it that you're going to her party."

"Oh, wouldn't miss it for the world," June answered.

"I didn't get an invitation," I said.

"We can remedy that. I'll take you as my plus one."

"Ellen Boudreaux is Ferrina's best friend. She'll be there."

June huffed, "All the more reason for you to show up looking fabulous."

"I can't, June. I don't have anything to wear. The police still have my Dior dress. Even if they gave it back, it's ruined."

"Don't you have a little black dress?"

"Yes, but I reserve it for funerals. I can't be seen gallivanting about wearing it at parties."

"Very well, then. You can choose one of my couture evening gowns. I'll even throw in some of my jewelry."

"To keep? You're the best." I just loved teasing June.

June blustered, "To borrow, you cheeky wench. And I want my dress back in the same condition as you took it and the same stones on my jewelry."

"Switch stones? Good lord. You must think I'm some international jewel thief."

At the mention of a jewel thief, June pursed her lips. "I wonder how Liam is doing? Does he think of me?"

Who is Liam, you ask? Liam was a thief posing as the valet for June's nephew, Anthony, who planned to steal and embezzle from June. To make a long story short, Anthony was thrown out of the Big House on his ear, but Liam was allowed to stay as Charles' under-butler. Charles loathed Liam, but June set out to reform Liam and eventually took him to her bed.

Yeah, I wince at the thought of those two together as well. The upshot was Liam did steal some fabulous gemstones, but not from June, and no one had seen him since. The scuttlebutt was that he sold the gems on the black market and was living like a king in Europe. Since the gems had been missing for decades, and the true owner, Bunny Witt, had been murdered, no one filed a police report on them. So they officially never existed. No crime had been committed. Liam was free as a bird.

June had been bereft ever since. She longed for her "girl toy."

"Didn't you date Ferrina's husband, King?" I said, changing the subject.

"I did for a very short time after my first husband had passed away. Oh, my word, King was tedious. I think one of the reasons I went to Europe was to flee him. He ended up marrying one of my good friends, and, of course, they divorced several years later. I can only imagine how my friend must have suffered from boredom. It was much later when King met Ferrina and married her. He must have been in his fifties then."

Amelia said, "Ferrina had a baby right quick, too."

"Babies are always an insurance policy for a woman in May-December marriages, especially if there is a prenup involved," June said.

"Yes. Babies. They certainly can upset the apple cart though," I mused, thinking about the documents Shelby Carpenter was carrying with him when he died—among other things.

"What does that mean?" Bess asked.

"Nothing. I think I'll go up and select a dress now."

"I mean it, Josiah. No rips. No tears. No stains or you'll pay to fix it."

"Yes, your majesty," I called over my shoulder, heading toward the elevator. I took it up to the second floor and entered June's glamorous bedroom with its metallic silver wallpaper with Chinese pink blossoms and a silver bedspread on her king bed. I entered June's massive closet, which was as big as my bedroom suite and began going through her evening gowns. The closet even had its own filtering system to keep dust off June's clothes.

June had grouped her gowns into eras. All the gowns purchased in the sixties were grouped together as well as those from the seventies, eighties, etc. You get the picture. I skipped looking at the seventies gowns. Nothing pretty came of the seventies, so I headed for the sixties era. Each gown was tagged with the date purchased, where June had worn it, and what jewelry accessorized it.

There was another reason I looked through the sixties gowns. June had shrunk with age, so her dresses had become more diminutive over time. I thought I had the best chance of finding a dress that would fit me from the sixties. I had shed quite a few pounds over several years, but I knew the gowns from the nineties were a lost cause even with my weight loss. As I went through the couture gowns, I hummed the theme song from *The Avengers*. What would Emma Peel wear?

Pulling out one gown after another, I almost despaired. I couldn't find a dress that would fit me nor something I liked. Apparently a lot of ugly dresses were made in the 1960s as well as the 1970s. Then I came across a little black number that reminded me of the dress Audrey Hepburn wore in the opening scene of *Breakfast At Tiffany's*. I pulled it out and looked in the full length mirror while holding the dress in front of me. It would do. Simple but elegant.

By that time Amelia had come upstairs and poked her head in the closet. "Need any help?"

"What do you think?" I held out the dress.

"Lady Elsmere hasn't worn that dress in decades. It goes well with your hair." She looked at the tag. "She last wore this dress for a New Year's Eve party in London. Just been gathering mothballs ever since. Glad to see you're going to take it out and give it a spin."

I looked back in the mirror, cocking my head from one side to another, trying to make up my mind. "Do you have any long black evening gloves to go with this?"

Amelia went over to a wall of drawers and rummaged through one. "These will do."

I put them on. "They're perfect, don't you think?"

Amelia nodded. "How are you going to wear your hair?"

"I was thinking an updo."

"Perfect for the era. What about jewelry?"

"Does June have a tiara comb?"

Amelia laughed. "You mean like the one Audrey Hepburn wore? Every white woman wants to look like Audrey Hepburn in *Breakfast At Tiffany's*. Are you going to a party or dressing up for Halloween?"

I grinned sheepishly and shrugged. "Guilty as charged."

Amelia patted my shoulder. "Let's see what we can find. June has a choker that I think would look splendid."

I spent the next hour trying on the dress with different pieces of June's jewelry and finally selected two pieces. The dress was very tight, so Amelia was going to let out the seams for me. We made a pact not to tell June about the alterations. June's good nature would only go so far, and altering her clothes did not fall under the rubric of "borrowing" a dress.

I left feeling lighter knowing my fairy godmother had come to my rescue and instead of cinders and soot, I could go to the ball with my head held high. Cinderella had nothing on me.

Other Books By Abigail Keam

Mona Moon Mysteries

Princess Maura Tales

Josiah Reynolds Mysteries

Last Chance For Love Series

About The Author

Hello, my friend. I hope you enjoyed *Death By Stalking*. I have such fun writing about Josiah and her quirky friends. If you like to read in other genres, I also write *The Princess Maura Tales*, a high fantasy series and *The Last Chance For Love Series*, a happily-ever-after sweet romance series. I would love to hear from you.

abigailshoney@windstream.net

If you like *Death By Stalking*, please leave a review and tell your friends about me.